DIAL (

Brent Bols

ᵇʸ

Michael Campling

The Awkward Squad

The Home of Picky Readers

All members receive a newsletter worth reading plus Compendium, a starter collection of exclusive previews. You'll also receive bonus content and advance notice of regular discounts and free books

Join at:

mikeycampling.com/freebooks

CAST OF CHARACTERS

On Earth

Brent Bolster - PI and member of the Association of Galactic Investigators (AGI).

Vince Claybourne – Assistant to Brent.

Maisie Richmond – A researcher employed by the UN.

Mayor Enderley – City Mayor.

Doctor Cooper – Scientist at GIT – the Gloabon Institute of Technology (an Earth institution funded by the Gloabons).

Dawson – A PI from what used to be London.

Dave Murphy – A security guard at the mayor's office.

Frank Deacon - A security guard at the mayor's office.

The Gloabons

Rawlgeeb – Liaison Officer in the Earth Liaison Unit (ELU).

Breamell – An administrator in the Sampling Records department.

Pentledaw – A senior colleague of Rawlgeeb in the ELU.

Clactonbury – A senior colleague of Rawlgeeb in the ELU.

Shappham – Head of the Sampling Records department.

Fleet Admiral Squernshall – Commanding Officer of *The Gamulon*, the Gloabon space station and Officer in Charge of the Gloabon Expeditionary Fleet. Also, Chair of the Earth Upgrade Committee.

Captain Zorello – Adjutant to Fleet Admiral Squernshall.

Commander Tsumper – A Gloabon officer with ambitions.

Surrana – Assassin and member of the Gloabon Guild of Assassins.

Beetfrump – An operative of the ELU.

Andelians

Officers and crew of *The Kreltonian Skull*.

Admiral Norph – Commanding Officer.

Commander Stanch – First Officer.

Zak3 – Science Officer. A cybonic lifeform.

Zeb – Science Officer. A cybonic lifeform.

Lieutenant Turm – Senior Navigation Officer.

Lieutenant Command Dex – Chief Engineer.

Petty Officer Harro – A Security Officer invented solely for the purposes of a dreadful pun.

Ensign Chudley – Communications Officer.

Lieutenant Grulb – The Ship's Counselor and therefore on the verge of nervous collapse.

Kreitians

Lord Pelligrew – Commanding Officer of *The Star of Kreit*, Pelligrew commands the Andel-Kreit Fleet.

CHAPTER 1

Earth

Brent Bolster opened his eyes and reached for the gun beneath his pillow. His bedroom, normally lit only by the intermittent scarlet glare from the neon barroom sign below his window, was bathed in an eerie green glow. *The alarm clock?* Brent's fingers closed around the polished steel butt of his old-fashioned pulse pistol. *Something isn't right.* For a start, he didn't have an alarm clock. He'd owned such a thing at one time, but now there was only a hunk of molten plastic on his nightstand. He'd had a difference of opinion with the device over the intricacies of the daylight saving system, and the clock hadn't glowed for a while; not since the flames went out anyhow. Brent closed his eyes. *Green glow—so what?* It was probably just one of his electronic devices letting him know it was still switched on, or maybe his handset needed recharging. The damned thing ate through carbon credits like they were going out of fashion. He let go of his pistol and rolled over onto his back, trying not to think about his next carbon bill. And someone cleared their throat.

Brent sat up straight, one hand sliding under the pillow. Where the hell was his pistol? He'd had it just one second ago. How could it be gone?

The alien standing beside his bed coughed politely. "Excuse me, but are you looking for something?"

"What the hell does it look like I'm doing?" Brent demanded. "Ah, what's the use?" He stopped searching and eyed the alien. The creature was a typical Gloabon: tall, at least six feet four, and humanoid with the usual complement of arms and legs. Its head was roughly egg-shaped, the bald dome of its smooth skull catching the glow from the computer tablet the creature held in its hand. But at least this alien was fully clothed: decked out in a pristine blue flight suit, the tight material emphasizing its angular body. Brent hated it when the Gloabons showed up naked; it was enough to put him off chorizo for life. "So, what do you mean by busting in here in the middle of the goddamned night? What do you want?"

The alien grinned, its pale lips pulling tight to reveal a row of pointed white teeth. "Honored Earthling, my name is Rawlgeeb, and I'm pleased to say that tonight, I shall be your abductor."

Brent groaned. "Not again." He patted his hand across the cluttered surface of his nightstand, receiving only a small electric shock from the ruins of his digital clock, but then his fingers closed on his wallet. He flipped it open and held it up for the alien to see. "Take a peek at that, asshole, then get the hell out of my apartment and don't come back."

Rawlgeeb leaned forward, craning his neck, the wrinkled skin growing tighter as his neck extended. "Yes, that's very impressive. Keep it up and you'll soon be able to claim a free hot beverage of your choice."

"What?" Brent rifled through his wallet, flipping through its array of plastic pockets. "Wrong damned card."

"Oh, I don't know," Rawlgeeb offered, retracting his neck. "I was quite impressed. You only need six more stamps and then you'll have your reward. Just think of it— cappuccino, latte, flat white. The choice is endless." He rubbed his hands together. "I'm rather fond of a double ristretto."

Brent gave him a side-eye. "I thought you, erm, beings, couldn't drink coffee."

"Technically we're not supposed to," Rawlgeeb said, a hint of sadness in his voice. "I mean, the caffeine is, well, it's a potent hallucinogen for us, but it's the taste that I can't resist. And the aroma. Ah, the scent of freshly roasted Arabica—there's nothing like it." He shrugged. "It's a shame it drives me out of my mind. The last time I had a Starbucks I was convinced I was being chased by an enormous dog. I've never run so fast in my life. Three days solid. By the time the coffee wore off, I was in the place they used to call Nebraska."

Brett grunted. "Same thing happened to me."

"Really?"

"Sure, except substitute coffee for bathtub bourbon, and Nebraska for a Norwegian fishing boat en route to the Newfoundland colonies."

"And the dog? What creature did you imagine was chasing you?"

"The hound was real, all right. A three-headed German shepherd. And on the other end of its leash was a nasty piece of work from the Irradiated Zone who'd somehow got the impression that I'd stolen his wife."

"And had you?"

Brent shrugged. "How the hell would I know? Weren't you listening when I told you about the bathtub gin?"

"Bourbon," Rawlgeeb corrected, sounding affronted.

"Bourbon, gin, how the hell would I remember what color it was? It was three days before I could feel my teeth again."

"Yes, it's a fair point I suppose." Rawlgeeb hesitated, mashing his lips together as if chewing back his words. But it wasn't long before his tongue won the battle. "Dammit though, the details are important. You see, I *was* listening. Listening very hard in point of fact. Local languages are a skill of mine. Not everyone picks up on Earth-based idioms, but I've made a study of them. I'm on the second year of the advanced soap opera course. And I was the highest in my cohort when we went through the level three sitcoms."

"Bazinga," Brent drawled.

Rawlgeeb raised his eyebrows. "We covered *The Big Bang Theory* in kindergarten. I'm afraid I never really enjoyed it."

"You and half the western hemisphere," Brent said distractedly. "Ah, here's the damned thing. It got stuck down behind my drivers' license." He pulled a plastic card from the wallet and brandished it triumphantly. "Read it and weep, my friend." He leaned forward, extending his arm. "Just don't do that thing with your neck again, all right? Gives me the creeps."

Rawlgeeb inclined his head to read the card. "Association of Galactic Investigators. I see."

"Good, so you can tick the box and put me down as immune from abduction, then you can head on out and pick on some other poor sap, okay?"

"Ordinarily, yes."

Brent frowned. "What's the problem? Which part of *immune from abduction* don't you understand? Go on, get! Vamoose! Scram!"

"That won't be possible I'm afraid," Rawlgeeb said, pulling a gleaming metal band from his breast pocket. "You see, that is a perfectly nice AGI card, although I must say the photo doesn't do you justice, but—"

"But nothing! I'm a member and that's an end to it. So

goodbye. It's been swell, really it has. We must get together for a drink sometime. Heck, maybe I'll buy you an espresso and you can take a trip to crazy town for the weekend, but you have to get the hell out of my apartment and let me sleep. Right now!"

Rawlgeeb took a step closer, towering over Brent. "As I inferred, I recognize your AGI card, but unfortunately for you, it expired last Tuesday, so as of now, you are fair game."

Brent fumbled for his bedside lamp and flicked the switch, then he turned the card around in his hands, studying both sides. "Oh for fuck's sake!"

"Quite so," Rawlgeeb said, stretching the metal band between his hands, his long fingers stroking its lustrous surface. "Now, in order to optimize your abduction experience, what kind of cabin would you prefer for the duration of your stay with us—probing or non-probing?"

Brent paled. "What?" He shook his head. "I mean, you can't be serious. I'm AGI. I must've made a mistake on the renewal, that's all. I've been with the AGI for six years. You can't just—" He broke off suddenly as Rawlgeeb leaned over him and moved the metal band far too close to Brent's throat. "Wait! What the hell is that thing?"

"Just a precaution," Rawlgeeb said. "We call it the restrictor. But you didn't answer my question, although–" He broke off to chortle under his breath. "Of course, all the cabins, or *cells* as we used to call them, are the same, and *everybody* gets the full probing treatment, but I thought I'd try out my little joke. I came up with it after studying an episode of *Friends* in our Academy of Human Interaction, although I can never quite get the intonation correct."

"Neither could Matt Le Blanc."

Rawlgeeb froze. "How can you say that? He was my favorite. His double entendres were perfect."

"In this academy of yours, did they by any chance show you *Joey*?"

"Of course not." Rawlgeeb regarded Brent with a weary frown. "You know, we may take people from their families and subject them to an agonizing series of brutal experiments before implanting radioactive probes in the back of their necks and controlling their minds, ultimately driving them to madness and a lingering death, but we're not *sadists*."

Brent blinked, his mind rebelling, refusing to believe, even for one second, that this clown was really proposing to snatch him. And Rawlgeeb seized his opportunity, snapping the band around Brent's throat.

"No!" Brent yelled. But no sound came from his throat. A tingling crackle of static electricity swept over his body, and before he could react, he was plunged into an icy darkness, his consciousness slipping away. *That's it*, he thought. *Now I'll never get that free americano.* And then the darkness took him.

CHAPTER 2

Gloabon Space Station *The Gamulon* - Earth Orbit

Commander Tsumper glanced over her shoulder, checking that the Fleet Admiral's Adjutant, Captain Zorello, wasn't looking her direction, then she straightened her uniform and pulled herself up to her full height. *I'm not the only female in the damned fleet,* she thought. *So how come the tunic never fits right?* She cleared her throat, and when Zorello looked up, she caught his eye. "Excuse me, Captain, but do you think the Fleet Admiral will be long?"

Zorello frowned. "Are we keeping you from something, Commander?"

Tsumper's lips were suddenly dry. "No, of course not. I stand ready to serve the admiral in any way that he might demand."

"Yes. Quite." Zorello's expression softened. "But I wouldn't say those exact words to the old man if I were you. No sense tempting providence if you know what I mean."

Tsumper blinked. "If you're trying to intimidate me, Captain, I must object. There is no mission too taxing for me to undertake. I am prepared to lay down my life in the service of the Gloabon Government."

"It wasn't your life I was worried about," Zorello said. He looked her up and down then turned his attention back to his workstation. "I'm sure he'll be here soon, and if I haven't finished these figures–" He broke off suddenly, his ear cocked. "Flek! Here he comes." He jumped to his feet, snapping to attention, his arm whipping toward his chest in a salute, and at the same moment, the door slid open and Fleet Admiral Squernshall strode in, his eyes roving across the room from beneath his bristly eyebrows.

Ugh! Tsumper thought. *Disgusting!* By nature, Gloabons were smooth-skinned, but ever since they'd arrived in Earth orbit, some senior officers had adorned their faces with follicular implants. The members of the Earth Upgrade Committee were especially keen on the trend, and during her last attendance at one of their meetings, Tsumper had been amazed at the bizarre collection of beards and mustaches on display; amazed and not a little nauseated. Now, the Fleet Admiral was waggling his obscene, bushy eyebrows at her, and with a start, she realized she'd been too shocked to salute. She raised her arm, clenching her fist and thumping it against her chest with such force that a cough rose in her throat, and she let out a muffled wheeze. "Fleet Admiral," she said hurriedly. "I am humbled to be called before you. Please be assured that I'm ready to serve you in—" She broke off as she caught Zorello grinning at her, but then she realized that her sentence hadn't made sense and added, "to serve you in due course, and in line with the goals, and, er, the noble aspirations of the Gloabon Government."

Squernshall let out a sigh, whispering something under his breath that sounded suspiciously like, "Not another bloody zealot." Then he pointed to his office door and said, "Inside. Now." He swept past her, and Tsumper followed in his wake, wrinkling her nose. What was that smell? Had the Fleet Admiral taken to using human cleaning products? *Surely not!*

"Remain standing," Squernshall said as he took his seat behind the vast alloy desk. Opening a drawer, he produced a slim tablet computer and ran his fingers over the screen before holding it up, the screen facing Tsumper. "Know what this is?"

Tsumper craned her neck forward, painfully aware of the clicking made by her cervical vertebrae. She frowned.

"An annual quota report." She met Squernshall's gaze. "At least, that's what it looks like at first glance. But…" She took a breath, marshaling her courage. She had a thorough understanding of the principals of honesty and integrity, but when it came to pointing out the errors of her commanding officers, she'd found it best if those particular principals were shifted discretely out the way until her compulsion to speak her mind had passed. And so far, it had worked. She was the highest-ranking female officer in the Gloabon Expeditionary Fleet, and she wasn't about to throw that achievement away any time soon; especially not over something as piffling as this administrative error. Yes, the quota report was a mess, but until she was absolutely sure that no blame could be attached to her, she'd keep quiet and wait to see what Squernshall had on his mind. "Yes. An annual quota report. That is my first impression."

"Come on," Squernshall grumbled, waving the tablet in front of her eyes. "You can do better than that. You're supposed to be some sort of whiz kid–that's what I was told. Hot stuff is our Commander Tsumper. Knows how to run things, how to get things done."

"Fleet Admiral, your faith in me is–"

Squernshall cut her short. "Tell me exactly what is wrong with this report, and then we'll see what you're made of. We'll see if you're up to the task I have in mind."

"Task?"

"Yes." Squernshall gave her a meaningful look. "An important task, completion of which may well confer certain advantages on the lucky officer in charge. Promotion, perhaps."

Tsumper forced a smile. Was Squernshall on the level, or was this a giant trap being laid before her feet? There were some in the fleet who'd love to see her go down in flames, and if she let her ambition overreach her abilities, it would be a short trip to the ultimate humiliation: exile on the planet below. *I should make an excuse and leave,* she decided. *No sense in getting in over my head.*

"Caution can be an asset in an officer," Squernshall went on, offering her the tablet, "but it can also be a crutch. Perhaps you're not ready for this task after all. What a pity. I was just thinking that the next logical step in your career would be the command of your own vessel. *Captain Tsumper.* It has a certain ring to it, does it not?"

In one motion, Tsumper snatched up the tablet and held it close to her eyes. "Firstly, the totals from each report only appear to reconcile, but the cross-reference codes are simply incorrect. Now, if this were only an isolated instance, then I might suggest a simple administrative error, but those adjustments have been manually inserted, and that points to a deliberate and systematic falsification of the figures. This report is fraudulent and requires immediate investigation."

"And why would someone file a fraudulent report, do you think?"

"Hard to say for sure," Tsumper began. "To be certain, someone would need to trace back through all the logs and rebuild the records from the raw data."

Squernshall waved his hand in the air, encouraging her to go on. "Just for the sake of argument, put forward a possible motive. Hypothesize."

Tsumper pursed her lips. "Someone covering their tracks. Perhaps an officer has been lax in his record keeping. All sampling missions should be logged and recorded. Date of mission, number of humans sampled, biometric data obtained, tracking codes, and finally, the date on which the samples are returned to Earth. It should all be reconciled against the quotas, but if the samples weren't logged correctly when they came in, the returns department would've picked up on the error, so I suggest that someone has tried to cover up their incompetence by falsifying the data *before* the return was made."

"Good try," Squernshall said, "but it doesn't hang together. The returns department wouldn't be so easily fooled. For each case, they'd see a human in front of them, and no amount of tampering with the data would make them ignore the evidence of their eyes."

"But that's just it," Tsumper said, her smile widening as the full implication of her discovery became clear. "These people aren't being returned–they're being recategorized." She held out the tablet, pointing to a column of data. "Here. This code means *miscellaneous livestock*. And this one stands for *mammal of unknown species and/or origin*. We get a lot of those from Australia. There's another code, here, *domesticated vertebrate of no known purpose*." She beamed. "On Earth, I believe they call them *cats* though we don't really know what that means."

Squernshall sat back, his bizarre eyebrows creeping up his brow as though attempting to escape. "You're sure about this? There are thousands of sample codes. You can't know them all."

"No," Tsumper admitted. "There are a few in the microbial category that I have trouble with, but as for the rest…well, it was a stretch to learn the five hundred new categories brought in by the Earth Upgrade Committee last month, but I'd say I know them pretty well." She shrugged. "It's a hobby."

"Is it?" Squernshall shook his head. "Things have certainly changed since I was a young commander. The only codes I ever learned were the access keys to the rear admiral's liquor store." He let out a bark of laughter. "Old Hagendorf. What a blowhard. I wonder whatever happened to him."

Tsumper glanced down at her shoes. "Rear Admiral Hagendorf was court martialed, sir. He was found guilty of bringing the Gloabon Government into disrepute, stripped of his rank, and exiled to Kamalon Three."

"Oh. That's a damned shame."

"Yes. He was a friend of my father. The rear admiral was a great Gloabon in his time, but it seems he'd become addicted to Brahmian Liquor. The evidence against him was overwhelming."

"Very sad." Squernshall ran his hands over his desk's smooth surface. "Of course, what I was saying a moment earlier about the, er, the access codes, that was merely a mild exaggeration for the sake of an anecdote. You know…banter. No need to take it literally."

"Yes, Admiral. I understand."

"It's certainly not the kind of remark that I'd like to hear repeated." He flashed Tsumper a shark-like smile. "I'd take that kind of thing personally if I were ever to hear of it happening. And I *would* hear about it, believe me."

Tsumper nodded. "Understood."

"Good." Squernshall clapped his hands together and jumped to his feet. "So, are you ready to take on your new mission, Commander?"

"Mission, Admiral? Sorry, but I'm not…what mission, exactly would that be?"

"To solve the mystery, of course," Squernshall said, beaming. "To find out what's happened to all the missing samples and bring the perpetrator to justice! I'm convinced that you're the right officer for the job."

"That's very flattering, sir, but–"

"I am right, aren't I? You *will* take on the job, won't you?"

Tsumper felt the blood drain from her cheeks. "Yes, Admiral. It goes without saying. It would be my pleasure. An honor."

"That's what I thought." Squernshall gestured toward the door. "I'll have all the relevant data transmitted to your account. Deal with this promptly, Commander, but keep this mission just between ourselves. No one else is to know anything about it. No one. Is that clear?"

"Yes, sir." Tsumper saluted. "Thank you, sir. I won't let you down."

The Fleet Admiral grinned. "You're damned right, you won't. Because if you do, there won't be much left of you to exile. But we'll manage, somehow, even if we have to stitch you back together first." He chuckled as though amused at his own turn of phrase. "You can go now, Tsumper. I look forward to receiving your preliminary findings by, let's see…I have dinner on Earth at seven, but there's golf with some chaps from the UN in the afternoon–that won't take long. I expect they'll let me win. As usual. So how about you'll have your report on my desk by three?"

"Three?" Tsumper asked, her voice wavering. "Is that station time?"

"No. Earth time. UTC." Squernshall shook his head. "The senior officers stopped using station time ages ago. Wake up, Tsumper. If you're going to be a captain, you'll need to up your game. And that means socially too. No more nights at home memorizing the handbook."

"Yes, sir. I mean, no sir." Tsumper tugged at the lower edge of her tunic which had chosen this moment to cling uncomfortably to her skin. "I'd better get to it."

"Yes. You are dismissed."

Tsumper turned smartly on her heel and marched out, striding past the admiral's adjutant without a glance. Strictly speaking, she should've acknowledged him with at least a polite nod, but military etiquette was the last thing on her mind, and just for once, the formalities could take a hike. She had bigger problems to deal with, and if she didn't complete this mission correctly, she may never need to salute again. Indeed, she may not be able to. She may not be able to do anything much at all.

CHAPTER 3

Aboard *The Kreltonian Skull* - Andromeda Class Battle Cruiser

Official Status: Assigned to Andel-Kreit Coalition Fleet.

Ship's Log: Routine Patrol of Sector Seven-B.

Admiral Norph paced the bridge, his hands clasped behind his back, his restless fingers rubbing his talons across his palms, the crooked claws scraping across the scales with an insistent scraping hiss.

The officers hunched over their consoles, their stubby fingers darting over the touch screens as they kept their heads firmly down, their thick-skinned brows furrowed in apparent concentration. All were fully occupied with their assigned tasks. All, that is, except for the science officer. Zak3 stood upright at his post, his head turning from side to side, a bemused smirk on his thin lips as he tracked the admiral's motion.

Norph halted abruptly and turned his gaze on Zak3, his rheumy eyes narrowed as he studied the science officer's expression. "Am I entertaining you, *Mister?*"

The silence on the bridge grew thick, the rest of the officers sitting rigid, their hands frozen over their screens. The ship's counselor, Lieutenant Grulb, closed his eyes. The only sound was the faint whir of the bridge's dehumidifiers. No one breathed.

But Zak3, for whom breathing was not an option, lifted his chin. "Only mildly, Admiral. I'm afraid that if entertainment was your intention, I must report that your performance was lacking a number of the essential elements."

"Really? Is that so?" Norph said slowly, his voice little more than a whisper. "Well, well, well. " He stepped close to Zak3, raising his gaze to look the tall science officer in the eye. "So, why then, would you happen to have that moronic grin on the lifeless abomination that passes for your face?" Norph raised his voice to a low growl. "Did you blow a circuit or something? Did you fuse the tiny part of your robotic mind that tells you how to treat your superior officers with some respect?"

Zak3's smile faded as he seemed to realize the gravity of his situation. "No, Admiral. My neural net is completely operational, and all my circuits are functioning perfectly. I was merely observing the stress patterns in the deck which seem to be caused by your repeated…" His voice trailed away and his eyes went to the bolt gun on Norph's belt, apparently hypnotized by the way Norph was stroking the weapon's gleaming handle. "I apologize, Admiral," Zak3 added, standing to attention. "No offense was intended. "It won't happen again, sir."

"Good. Good." Norph stepped even closer to the hapless science officer. "That's all right then. We'll say no more about it." He smiled, but just as Zak3's shoulders relaxed, Norph whipped his bolt gun from its holster and aimed it at the science officer's head. "But that doesn't mean I'm not going to *do* something about it. And unfortunately for you, if there's one thing I can't stand, it's a smart-ass robot."

Zak3's lips worked silently for a second, then: "Sir, I respectfully remind you that I am not, in fact, a robot but a cybonic lifeform with the same rights as any serving officer in the Andel-Kreit fleet."

"Noted," Norph said, his thumb turning the slider on his bolt gun, switching it from automatic to single shot. "One bolt should do the job, don't you think?"

"Yes, Admiral," Zak replied. "But I calculate that the bolt

would pass through my skull and cause considerable damage to the critical systems on the bridge."

Norph nodded thoughtfully. "Good point." He lowered his aim until the gun pointed squarely at Zak3's chest, and when he pulled the trigger, the sharp crack of his weapon echoed through the bridge. For a moment, Zak3 rocked back on his heels, blinking rapidly, then his body slumped and he crumpled to the deck, his sturdy frame meeting the floor with a hollow thud.

Norph smiled as he holstered his weapon. "Right, that's the personnel well-being consultation dispensed with for the day." He paused to brush his hands together while mentally running down his to-do list. He'd already had a couple of crew members thrown in the brig for minor infringements of the uniform regs, and he'd breakfasted well enough, despite the inferiority of the Kreitian blood sausage. What was next? *Ah, yes*, he thought. *Start a war*. He turned to address the officers. "Listen up! We've been cooling our heels in this backward sector for far too long. We're heading out. We have a bold new mission with new objectives, and finally, some action. Are you ready?"

A chorus of agreement rang out: "Aye, aye, Admiral."

"Excellent." Norph swaggered across to his chair and sat down heavily, the seat's heavy-duty springs groaning in protest beneath his bulk. Norph made himself comfortable then tapped the console attached to the seat's armrest, his lips moving as he typed. Satisfied, he ran his tongue across his bared teeth then sat back, his eyes alight with a savage greed. "Helm, I've sent you a set of coordinates. Lay in a course and get us there as fast as you can. And on arrival, I want us fully cloaked."

Lieutenant Turm, the ship's senior navigation officer, activated her nav panel and went into action at the helm. "Aye,

Admiral. Laying in new course now. Setting cloak for automatic deployment."

"Good." Norph chuckled under his breath. "Number One, what's our travel time?"

The first officer, Commander Stanch, ran a hand across his brow as he studied his console. "Admiral, please be advised that those coordinates will take us very close to Earth. And under the terms of the Andel-Kreit treaty with the Gloabons–"

"Gloabons be damned!" Norph roared. "I don't give a flek for the knock-kneed coalition and the Kreitians' cozy little treaties. As of now, we fly under the colors of Andel as is our sovereign right. And we're not headed *toward* Earth, we're headed *to* Earth. Is that understood?"

"Yes, Admiral," Stanch said, his tone and manner brisk; a professional to the core. "In that case, our journey time will be just under thirteen hours."

Norph turned in his seat to glare at his first officer. "Is that in Andelian hours or Kreitian hours?"

"Standard Imperial Andelian hours, of course, sir," Stanch replied. "In fact, Admiral, with your permission, I'll switch ship-wide systems to run solely on Andelian units of measurement with immediate effect."

"Very good," Norph said, looking pointedly at the bridge's central clock, its numbers flashing past rapidly as it registered the miniscule units of time peculiar to the Kreitian system of timekeeping. Ever since the formation of the coalition, the entire fleet had been forced to adopt the nit-picking ways of the Kreitians, and he hated it; hated it with a passion bordering on insanity. And the ship's central clock, with its integrated system for time-stamping every damned thing he did, was a symbol of all that he despised.

But all that was about to change. With one command, he would be free. He gestured toward the clock, his hand chopping the air, and said, "Make it slow."

"Consider it done, Admiral," Stanch replied. "Sir, may I request the objective of our mission to Earth?"

"Oh, it's very simple," Norph replied, relaxing back into his chair and activating the hydraulic footrests. Tipping the seat back, he smiled up at the ceiling, absent-mindedly rubbing his stomach. "We're going to Earth because I'm hungry. Very hungry indeed."

CHAPTER 4

Gloabon Space Station *The Gamulon* - Earth Orbit

When Brent came around, the world was a blurred muddle of soft shapes in muted colors. He rubbed his face with both hands, scraping the dried mucus from the corners of his eyes, but it didn't make much difference. "Goddamned alien," he muttered. "He must've sucker punched me, knocked me out cold." He sat up, running his hands over the thin mattress beneath him. Wait. This wasn't his bed, was it? He squeezed his eyes tight shut and pinched the bridge of his nose, trying to force his throbbing headache into submission. It almost worked, and when he opened his eyes, the room resolved into a gloomy cell, its only exit a barred door, and its bare, steel-plated walls spattered with smeared stains. *I sincerely hope that's blood*, he thought, and his brain stopped backpedaling furiously and took a faltering step forward. He hadn't been hit, but abducted; zipped from his home and dropped into this filthy dump.

His hands went to his throat, but the restrictor collar had been removed. "That's something," he mumbled.

"What is?"

Brent leaped to his feet, his bleary eyes searching the shadows, but the only light came from the fitful glow beyond the barred door, and the far end of the cell was swathed in darkness. "Who's there? Come out!"

"Stay calm, cowboy," a soft voice purred, and slowly, a dark shape detached itself from the shadows. "My, you're a delight first thing in the morning, aren't you?"

Brent squared his shoulders and sucked in his stomach. The woman was tall with the build of an athlete, and yet somehow impossibly elegant. Her long, dark hair fell in loose curls around her face in a way that accentuated her finely sculpted cheekbones and dangerously dark eyes. Her dress was long and full, the bodice clinging subtly to her upper body, and the skirt's generous folds hinting at the length of the woman's legs. The dress was cut from a silky fabric with an almost undetectable sheen, and its color was a shade of indigo so deep that it seemed to have been spun from the purest moonlit sky of a midwinter night. The cell was bleak and badly lit, but the woman, just by taking a few steps, dispelled the gloom and sent the shadows scuttling for the farthest corners of the room. She was a vision of beauty; a wondrous apparition.

And by some miracle, Brent managed to stick out his hand and say, "Brent. Brent Bolster, private investigator."

The woman stepped closer; close enough for Brent to inhale a trace of her perfume, the delicate scent setting his senses on fire and giving his libido a gentle kick in the coccyx. She took his hand, her grip firm, her palm perfectly dry, and as she shook his hand, she looked him squarely in the eye. "Brent," she said. "Like the oil."

"Pardon me?" Brent felt his jaw drop slightly, and he knew that he must look like a buffoon, but for some unaccountable reason, there wasn't a damned thing he could do about it; his motor control, usually lightning fast, had abandoned him completely. "Olive?" he offered. "Sunflower?"

"Crude." She let go of his hand and laughed, the sound as soft as a tigress licking the ears of her favorite cub. "Brent crude. It's a type of oil. Well, it was, back when there was such a thing."

"Right. It was a joke. Yeah, I get it. I never heard that one before." Brent forced a crooked smile and tried to change tack. "You threw me there for a second, talking about oil, on account of how you don't look old enough to remember it.

Those were the days, huh?"

"Not really," she said, her expression suddenly serious. "Climate change, floods, droughts, and crop failure. What was your favorite part? Did you prefer the food riots or the were the civil wars more your cup of tea?"

Brent ran his hand across his jaw. "Well, forgive me. I was just trying to pay you a compliment, lady."

"It backfired." She smiled sweetly, adding, "And just for the record, I'm not old enough to remember fossil fuels, but a degree in geopolitics and a masters in economics tends to give me a certain perspective."

"No kidding. Listen, er, you never did tell me your name. And I need to know what to call you if we're ever going to bust the hell out of here."

She arched her eyebrows in surprise. "Maisie. Maisie Richmond. And what did you mean about *busting out?*"

Brent gave her an appraising glance. Maisie was clearly very beautiful, smart, and quick-witted, but she was out of his league, and unfortunately, she knew it. Any attempt at smooth talk would be a waste of time, and while her appearance had made him forget his headache for a few minutes, the throbbing pain had already returned to his temples with a vengeance. He'd had enough headaches to know that this one was planting a flag in his skull and making itself at home; it was here for the long haul, and nothing short of a lobotomy could persuade it to leave until it was good and ready. So when he spoke, he adopted a mocking tone, not caring whether she took offense or not. "*Busting out* is a colloquial expression much favored by those of us with a tendency to find themselves afflicted by adverse circumstances. For instance, it's the kind of thing I might say when locked in some lousy alien cell with a poor little rich girl."

Maisie bridled. *"Rich?* Who said anything about being rich?"

"Oh please, we're already cramped in here, there's no room for your sense of entitlement."

"To hell with you! I work for a living."

Brent looked her up and down. "Don't tell me–you're a roustabout and it's bring-your-own-ballgown day up on the space docks."

Maisie ran her hands defensively over her dress. "If you must know, I'm a researcher working for the UN, and I just happened to be on my way home from a fundraiser when I was taken."

"The UN is throwing a party to raise some cash? Jeez, things are worse than I thought. Didn't our green friends pay out enough backhanders this month?"

"For God's sake! You have absolutely no idea what the hell you're talking about. The UN is a fine organization, completely independent from the Gloabons. And the only money we were trying to raise was for a charity that's close to my heart." She hesitated. "Someone has to look out for the alligators. Since the Gloabons came…" She sniffed, dabbing at the corners of her eyes with her knuckles.

Gators! Brent thought. *The Gloabons can eat every last one of the little suckers and good luck to their digestive tracts.* But he regarded Maisie in silence for a while. Maybe she wasn't such a bad kid after all. Her heart was in the right place, and if he was any judge, every other part of her body was *exactly* where he liked it. Maybe he ought to cut her a little slack. He rummaged in his pocket and retrieved a packet of tissues. "Here," he said, offering her the whole pack. "Don't worry, they're clean."

"Thanks." Maisie took the pack and pulled out a tissue,

wiping her eyes and blowing her nose. "These smell funny."

"Antiseptic. Antibacterial. Antiviral. Anti-pretty-much-everything. They're made especially for off-world military types. The grunts call them bio-wipes. They tried the name *standard issue tissue*, but it never caught on." Brent flashed her a smile; her cue to be impressed by his witty wordplay, but she didn't bite. "Anyhow, they're very effective. Very absorbent. Good for plugging bullet wounds, although I got that pack from a friend after they went past their expiry date, so I wouldn't bet your life they still work. Should be fine though. Probably."

"Right. I'll take your word for it." She passed the packet back to him.

"It's all right. You can keep them. You never know when they might come in handy."

"Thanks, but I wouldn't want to deprive you." Maisie thrust the packet at him. "Please. I insist."

"Fair enough." Brent took the bio-wipes and pocketed them. "Probably just as well. There's a chance they're a little radioactive right now. They get that way once the isotopes break down or something." He caught the full force of Maisie's incredulous glare and shrugged his shoulders. "It's all cool. Nothing to worry about."

Maisie pursed her lips then crossed the room, putting some distance between them. She leaned her back against the wall and stared into the middle distance, her expression blank.

I get the message, Brent thought, and he made a move of his own, strolling up to the door and wrapping his hands around two of the bars, giving them an experimental tug. The bars were solid steel, over an inch thick and firmly welded in place. *Old Earth tech,* he thought. *Practically antique. I would've expected something fancier.* The prison cell was like something from an old movie. There wasn't even an electronic lock on the door, just a simple handle and a hole for an old-fashioned key. Brent tried the handle, willing it to turn. He could almost hear the satisfying clunk it would make; the slow groan from the hinges as he swung the door open; the hug Maisie would give him when he set her free.

"Goddammit!" The handle wouldn't budge, and his daydream came crashing down. "Right. New plan needed."

Maisie let out a snort. "That was your first plan? To stroll up and open the door? Didn't you think I'd have tried that already?"

"Never overlook the obvious," Brent said. "It's often the simplest things that come through."

"Lucky for you."

"Right." Brent nodded then realized she'd just insulted him. "Very funny. But at least I'm taking a look around. It's got to be better than just standing there waiting for the green guys to come and take us."

"Whatever." Maisie heaved a sigh. "I wouldn't make too much noise though. There was a guy in here earlier, and while you were sleeping it off, he kicked up a fuss. He screamed, shouted, kicked the door. They didn't like it."

"What happened?"

Maisie pushed herself off from the wall and walked slowly toward him. "Take a guess. Do you see him here?"

"They came for him."

"Three of them. Armed with those shiny pistols they have."

"Parton guns," Brent said. "Kind of a ray gun. They might look like toys, but they pack a punch you wouldn't

25

believe. So much as touch that beam with your pinkie and all of a sudden you can only count up to nine."

Maisie looked down her nose at him, her eyes cold. "They didn't fire a shot. The guy took one look at them and went down on his knees, begging for his life. But they just took him. Picked him up and dragged him away. And from the look on their faces, I'd guess they weren't taking him out for ice cream."

Brent set his jaw. There wouldn't be much he could do if three goons armed with parton guns came to grab him, but he'd be damned if he'd go without putting up a fight. "How about this. You go to the back and pretend to be sick. Make like you're throwing up or something. I'll stand all quiet, and when they come in, I'll jump them."

"It won't work," Maisie said. "The Gloabons are too cautious to be taken in by such a simple trick. And anyway, I think it's too late."

"What do you mean?" Brent asked. But he didn't wait for a reply. He cocked his ear and knew exactly what Maisie had just heard. Beyond the door, an unmistakable sound reverberated along the bleak corridor, the noise echoing from the smooth metal walls: the rigid rhythm of boots thudding against the floor. *At least three goons*, Brent decided. *Maybe more.* And there was no doubt about which direction the Gloabon troops were marching. The sound grew steadily louder, thundering through the forbidding corridor, every pounding footstep vibrating in Brent's chest. They were coming, and since Brent had heard no trace of any other prisoners nearby, he knew they were coming for him.

CHAPTER 5

Gloabon Space Station *The Gamulon* - Earth Orbit

The communal bath on the leisure deck was less crowded than usual, but Rawlgeeb tried to hide his disappointment. He skirted around the bathing areas favored by the military types and made his way over to the corner frequented by his fellow members of the Earth Liaison Unit. On the station, there were very few areas reserved for civilians like Rawlgeeb, but the military officers seemed to prefer the company of their peers, and in most communal areas an unspoken division had occurred, the boundaries between civilian and military not fixed, but on any given occasion, generally distinct. The only exceptions were the canteens, where etiquette demanded that all crew members were seated in order of arrival, and rank was forgotten for the brief time it took to catch and consume the reptile of the day.

As he approached the bath, Rawlgeeb wondered what might be served for lunch later in the day. He'd had a long night down on Earth, then he'd worked until morning to complete the records for his latest batch of human samples, and all he'd managed to grab for breakfast was a small garter snake from one of the vending machines. The creature had been chilled into a torpor, barely alive, and he hadn't enjoyed it at all. *Not even a lizard*, he thought bitterly. *You'd think they could rustle up something with legs.* But his hunger would have to wait. Trips to Earth always left him feeling unclean, the stink of the place clinging to him long after he'd returned to the ship, and he needed a bath to make him feel Gloabon again.

He slipped out of his red bathrobe and tossed it on a chair, then he made his way slowly down the slippery steps into the water, sinking beneath the thick layer of dark green foam that frothed and churned on the surface. *That's better*. He could almost feel the bacteria soaking into his skin. He lifted his arm, the viscous bath water trickling slowly through his fingers, and he was pleased to see that already his skin was regaining its deep, lustrous sheen as the bacteria colonized the cells of his epidermis. He waded across the bath to the seating area and squeezed onto a ledge between a couple of the senior administrators from the office. Technically, Pentledaw and Clactonbury were Rawlgeeb's superiors, but in the communal bath that wouldn't matter, and anyway, both looked to be at their most relaxed, as if they'd been soaking for hours, their flesh swollen and puffy. The three Gloabons acknowledged each other with polite nods, then Rawlgeeb sat back on the smooth marble ledge and relaxed, his muscles loosening as the warm water did its work. A smile spread slowly across his face, and he closed his eyes.

"Hey, Rawlgeeb," Pentledaw said, his monotonous voice laced with a North American accent, an affectation, in Rawlgeeb's opinion, adopted by far too many in the office. "Are you doing what I think you're doing?"

Rawlgeeb opened one eye and regarded his companion. "What?"

"Did you pee in the bath?" Clactonbury demanded.

"No." Rawlgeeb opened his other eye and shifted his position. "Give me a break, guys. I've only just got in."

"Well, could you hurry up and get on with it?" Pentledaw asked. "The glyphoforms won't feed themselves you know, and my nose says the ammonia content in this place is getting low."

"All right," Rawlgeeb replied. "I'll do it in a minute." He looked from Clactonbury to Pentledaw and back again. "Seriously? Are you going to stare at me until I pee?"

Clactonbury frowned. "What's wrong with that?"

"Yeah, what's the problem?" Pentledaw chipped in. "Are you trying to say something?"

Rawlgeeb held up his hands in mock surrender. "No, of course not. It's just, with you two looking at me, I don't think I can go. You know, not on demand."

Pentledaw's face fell. "That's…weird."

"Is it?" Rawlgeeb asked, his voice choosing this moment to adopt a higher pitch. "I mean, it's just a reflex or something."

"Yew!" Clactonbury wrinkled his nose. "You know what you sound like?"

Rawlgeeb pursed his lips. "Don't. Not after the night I've just had. Just…don't go there."

But Clactonbury was not to be denied his moment of fun. "You sound like a flecking *human.*" His companions stared at him for a second, their gently steaming faces twisted in horror, and Rawlgeeb swallowed hard.

They're right, a small voice whispered in the back of Rawlgeeb's mind. *You're not the Gloabon you used to be.* He shook his head. "That's not fair. It's slander, that's what it is. Racial harassment. I could report you for that." He tried to look his coworkers in the eye and almost succeeded. "Also, it's…it's just plain bad manners."

Clactonbury stared at him, aghast, his mouth open. But then his expression creased, and he collapsed into raucous laughter, Pentledaw joining in.

"We got you there," Clactonbury crowed. "Dude, you should've seen your face."

"Perfect," Pentledaw chortled. "I wish I had a vid clip of that one."

Rawlgeeb sighed. "Oh, very good. Yeah, I get it. Boy, I

fell for that one, didn't I?"

Clactonbury slapped him on the shoulder. "Aw, you're a good sport, Rawlgeeb. I'll give you that."

"Thanks," Rawlgeeb said, forcing a humorless chuckle from his lips. He opened his eyes comically wide and stared into the distance. "Guess what—that was so funny I just peed."

Pentledaw hooted with laughter. "Well done, my friend. You're a star."

"I try," Rawlgeeb said. "I do my best."

Pentledaw bowed his head in mock solemnity. "The glyphoforms thank you for your contribution." Smirking, he scooped up a handful of water and splashed it over his face. "Lovely."

Clactonbury sighed. "Pent, my old friend, I guess we should be heading back to work."

"I guess so," Pentledaw replied. He sighed and stood, waiting for Clactonbury to join him. "You know what, Rawlgeeb? Some of the guys are heading down to the planet for a drink after work. Why don't you tag along with us?"

Rawlgeeb blinked. "Really?"

"Sure," Clactonbury said. "Why not? Everybody needs a little downtime, right?"

"Yes, of course," Rawlgeeb said, "but I was going to work on my sitcoms tonight. There are so many episodes of *Frasier*, and if I'm honest, I'm struggling with Daphne's accent." His coworkers stared at him, and he knew that he should shut up, but for some reason, he couldn't. "I mean, who talks like that? Is it a joke or what? She's supposed to be from England, but her brothers all seem to have different accents. I tried cross-referencing it with *Coronation Street*, that's an old English soap opera, but I didn't...I didn't come up with anything…" He let his voice trail away, leaving only an embarrassed silence hanging in the steamy air.

Clactonbury exchanged a look with Pentledaw then said, "Listen, Rawlgeeb, if you don't want to come along, just say. We won't be offended."

Pentledaw nodded. "It's no problem." He paused. "Although, if you want to talk about it, *I'm listening*."

The pair erupted into a laughing fit. "That's priceless," Clactonbury said. "Your timing was perfect."

"Thanks." Pentledaw wiped a tear from his eye. "You know, Rawlgeeb, I specialized in *Frasier* in my third year. I got pretty good marks too, so if you come along tonight, I'll help you out. Deal?"

"Oh," Rawlgeeb replied. "Oh, that's very kind of you. Really." He smiled. "Thank you. Where are you meeting?"

"Oh, we generally zing straight down to the planet and hang out in the arrivals lounge for a couple of looseners before we venture farther out," Pentledaw said. "We'll finish work early, say eight o'clock, and you can meet us in the lounge. Sound good?"

"Yes. Eight o'clock." Rawlgeeb nodded vigorously, picturing his workload and wondering how he was going to get through it by midnight, never mind eight o'clock. "Was that, eight o'clock sharp or later, like maybe eight thirty?" he asked hopefully.

Pentledaw laughed. "Just somewhere *around* eight. We won't quibble over a minute or two. Like I said, we'll meet up in arrivals. No need to look so worried, Rawlgeeb. Oh, dude, you crack me up, you really do."

"Right." Rawlgeeb made to get up.

"Where are you going?" Clactonbury asked. "You only just got in. Your cells won't be fully colonized for another hour at least."

"That's right," Pentledaw added. "If you're going to come out with us, we need you at your best. There might be some girls from accounting in the bar, and you know what they say…"

Clactonbury finished the sentence, "Show 'em some green, to keep them keen." He gave Rawlgeeb a broad grin. "Know what I'm saying?"

Rawlgeeb did his best to return the smile. "Yes. There I go again. Silly me." He sat back. "I'll see you at eight. On the dot."

"*Around* eight," Pentledaw said, then they moved away, wading through the water and chatting quietly. Rawlgeeb thought Clactonbury said the word *Niles*, and Pentledaw cackled, patting his friend on the back. *What have I done?* Rawlgeeb asked himself. *I'm going to look a complete fool.* He closed his eyes and massaged his temples with his fingertips.

Within the strict hierarchy of the civil service, Pentledaw and Clactonbury were many ranks above Rawlgeeb, so it was flattering that they'd asked him out. It was a wonderful opportunity for him to impress them, and if all went well, it could be fantastic for his career. *Unless you make a complete idiot of yourself,* the small voice in Rawlgeeb's mind whispered. *Unless you offend them, or let yourself down, or appear ignorant of Earth customs, or…* He sat bolt upright, his eyes wide open. What if they talked about sport? Or, even worse, what if they asked him about American sports? He'd done the basics, like everyone else, but in his first year, he'd been ambitious. Everyone else had chosen the common sports for their in-depth studies, but he'd wanted to challenge himself. *Cricket,* he thought miserably. *Why on Earth did I choose cricket?* He threw back his head and stared up through the swirling clouds of steam. He knew what was meant by *silly mid-on* and *LBW*. He knew what a leg break was, and he even understood some of the finer points of the bizarre etiquette surrounding the game. But none of this had ever come up in conversation. Not once. *Oh well, it's only a night out*, he thought, closing his eyes. *How bad can it be? What could possibly go wrong? I've had a great day. I'm on a roll. Success is within my grasp. All will be well. All* will *be well.*

"Excuse me, Rawlgeeb? It is Rawlgeeb, isn't it?"

Rawlgeeb sat up with a start, glaring at the young female standing by the bath. "What the hell do you think you're doing, creeping up on me like that?"

The female's hands fluttered in front of her stomach. She was obviously a junior administrator; her drab clothing was cheap and ill-fitting. And that was another reason for him to be angry with her: what the hell was she thinking, going into the baths fully clothed for flek's sake? "This is outrageous," Rawlgeeb fumed. "Just tell me what you want and then get out of here. Come on! Spit it out!"

The female goggled at him. "Spit? Spit where? I don't understand. You want me to spit in the bath?"

Rawlgeeb let out a groan of frustration. "I don't know what they teach in the academy these days, but *spit it out* is a human expression. It means that you should spit your words out, that is, you should come to point and state your business. Unfortunately, on this occasion, it appears to have had the opposite effect."

The female nodded sadly, her eyes downcast. "I'm sorry, Rawlgeeb, sir. I do try to keep up with the idioms, but I'm always putting my elbow in my mouth."

Rawlgeeb took a deep breath. The female was perhaps younger than he'd first thought, and she was nervous at having been sent to speak to him. He was, after all, an experienced liaison officer, and at least twelve grades above an office junior. *Probably in awe of me*, he decided. *I was much the same at her age.* He favored her with a smile, realizing that she was actually quite attractive. Her demure manner certainly made a refreshing change from the frosty, no-nonsense attitude he usually got from his female colleagues. "Let's start over. Yes, I am Rawlgeeb. No doubt you recognized me immediately. And you are?"

"Breamell. I'm from the records office."

"I see. So tell me, Breamell, what brings you here today?"

Breamell licked her lips. "I was sent here, sir, by Shappham–he's the chief administrator in the Sampling Records department."

"Oh, I know who Shappham is. Who doesn't?" Rawlgeeb frowned. Strictly speaking, Shappham wasn't his boss; the Earth Liaison Unit was meant to be independent of the record-keeping arm of the administration. But Shappham had spent years building the department of Sampling Records into his personal kingdom, and he threw his weight about at every opportunity, stirring up trouble for others whenever he could, then stepping back to enjoy the ensuing chaos, all the while watching for chances to advance his own career. So whatever message Breamell had brought, it probably wasn't going to be good news, and it was almost certainly going to cause a great deal of paperwork. "All right, you'd better tell me what he wants. Let's get it over with. What's happened?"

"Er, I'm afraid there's a problem." Breamell bit her lower lip in a fetching fashion. "It's some of the samples you brought up today. New facts have come to light, and it seems that there has been an error. The details were sent to your account, but you didn't reply, so they sent me to find you. I thought you must be somewhere without your tablet, and there's only really one place where that might be the case, so here I am."

"There's been an error? What kind of error?" Rawlgeeb let out a dismissive grunt. "I don't make errors. I follow the regulations to a *T*."

A flicker of confusion clouded Breamell's expression.

"*To a T* means I follow the rules precisely as laid down," Rawlgeeb said patiently. "No one is more careful than me. No one."

"I'm sure that's true, sir, but nevertheless, an error has occurred, and Shappham said that as the liaison officer responsible for obtaining the incorrect samples, he'd be grateful if you would solve the problem at your earliest convenience."

"Shappham said that? He said he'd be grateful?"

Breamell broke eye contact for a moment. "I'm paraphrasing. I can't recall his exact words. There was a lot of shouting. And swearing. And some projectiles." She hesitated. "So, can I tell him that you'll deal with it? I do hope so, because, if you aren't going to fix it, I'll have to go back to Shappham with the bad news, and he's not going to be happy."

Rawlgeeb waited until Breamell looked back at him then said, "Of course I'll deal with it. Leave it with me."

"Oh, thank you, sir."

"Think nothing of it," Rawlgeeb said smoothly, "Tell me, Breamell, do you ever get down to Earth?"

She rolled her eyes. "With my workload? Chance would be a fine thing."

"Really, that's too bad. A young person like you…you

should be broadening your horizons." He gave her his most winsome smile. "When I've dealt with this little sampling problem and tidied up a few other important matters, I'll be heading down to the planet. Why don't you come with me? I could show you around."

Breamell bobbed up and down in excitement. "Really? Wow! That would be amazing. But...but...I'm not sure if I should."

"Come on. It's all above board. We'll be joining some of my colleagues. In fact, it's a good opportunity for you to meet some important members of the Earth Liaison Unit. Think of it as a chance to do a bit of networking."

"In that case, yes. Yes, please! I'd be delighted. What time? Where shall I meet you?"

"I'll swing by and pick you up. I'm sure I can find your quarters. I'll be there at eight...that is *around* eight. All right?"

"Yes. Thank you. I'd better get back to work." She started to walk away, then half-turned and flashed him a grateful smile.

Rawlgeeb watched her leave. *Take that Clactonbury and Pentledaw!* he thought. *I'm bringing a date!* He rubbed his hands together then pushed himself up from the water. First, he'd grab his tablet and deal with this administrative cockup, and then he'd go and power through his workload in record time. After that, he was damned well going to go out and enjoy himself. After the day he'd had, he was entitled to an evening off. Frankly, he'd earned it.

CHAPTER 6

Aboard *The Kreltonian Skull* - Andromeda Class Battle Cruiser.

Official Status: Listed as Missing.

Ship's Log: En route to Earth.

Chief Engineer Dex stared down at the cybonic lifeform on his bench and let out a long and heartfelt sigh. "Zak3, what the hell did he do to you?"

At Dex's side, Lieutenant Turm shook her head. "I brought him down as soon as I could. Do you think you can fix him up?"

"He wasn't a goddamned robot, he was a cybonic lifeform." Dex gestured angrily toward the bench. "He's not broken, he's *dead*. And I'm a technician, not a witch doctor."

"I'm sorry, but you know how it is. We're short of a science officer, and that's not good for any of us. Especially with the old man going off the rails like this." Turm wrung her hands together. "There must be *something* you can do. You keep this old ship running as smooth as if it were built yesterday. *The miracle worker*, that's what we call you on the bridge."

Dex allowed himself a grim smile. *"Miracle worker! That's about right. You should see the main reactor–I've got it bypassed like a Klumzel tree. Sometimes I wonder if the engines can take it."*

"But they do. And that's down to you." Turm slapped him on the back. "Come on, Dex. See what you can do. And look on the bright side–at least he didn't shoot this one in the head."

"I suppose that's something. It's a damned sight more

than I can say for the poor devils who came before him." Dex scratched at his chin, his talons tugging at the flesh along his jawline. "You say Zak3 *knew* he was about to get shot?"

"Yes. It wasn't pretty, but he knew all right. There was just nothing we could do to save him."

"I wonder," Dex murmured.

"What is it?"

"Well, if he had time, there's a chance he performed an emergency backup of his neural net, transferring the data to his internal backup site."

"Does that mean you might be able to bring him back?" Turm asked.

Dex tilted his head to one side. "Like I said, there's a chance. I might be able to recover his neural pathways completely, but equally, there's a distinct possibility that his mind will be at least partially corrupted."

"That doesn't sound great," Turm said. "If his brain is scrambled, I don't see how he could function as a science officer."

"That's not the problem. His functional protocols are relatively stable–they should be easy to recover."

"So, what's the problem?" Turm asked.

"It's his *mind* I'm worried about." Dex intoned. "He won't be Zak3 anymore, not as we knew him. But as for what he might become…I'm just not sure. I'm not sure at all."

CHAPTER 7

Gloabon Space Station *The Gamulon* - Earth Orbit

Brent leaned against the bars of the cell door and studied the trio of Gloabons who'd come to a halt on the other side. "Well, if it isn't my favorite coffee lover," he said. "Did you miss me?"

Rawlgeeb, flanked by two burly guards, scowled. "You! I might've known you'd be the cause of all this trouble."

"Aw, don't be like that," Brent replied. "I thought we were getting along just swell back on Earth. But then everything went sour. I mean, you didn't even tuck me in last night. No goodnight kiss. Nothing. I'm starting to wonder if you care about me at all."

"Be silent!" Rawlgeeb ordered, his facial features performing a strange dance, creating an expression Brent had never seen on a Gloabon before. And the armed guards were casting strange looks at each other behind Rawlgeeb's back. *Attaboy, Rawlgeeb,* Brent thought. *Keep on getting het up while I needle you some more.* It was only a matter of time before the alien lost his temper and made a mistake, and Brent was ready to seize whatever advantage he could take.

"There's no need to shout." Brent shook his head sadly. "You know, this is really disappointing, Rawlplug. It takes two to make a relationship work, and clear lines of communication are very important. Perhaps we ought to visit that counselor we talked about. I think you have some unresolved issues, and it does no good to bottle them up."

"Shut up and listen!" Rawlgeeb snapped, his voice cracking. He held up a tablet computer, brandishing it in Brent's face. "My name is *Rawlgeeb,* and you will listen to what I have to say in silence, or I'll have my colleagues start lopping off limbs until you pay attention. Is that clear?"

Brent affected a Gallic shrug. "I was only trying to help, but let's play it your way and see how it goes."

"Good. This document is my authorization to return you to your planet immediately. You will not take part in our sampling process, and your details will be struck from the records. In addition, in recompense for any inconvenience in your abduction, a sum of one thousand credits will be paid into your personal account, provided of course that you do not pursue any further claim against the Gloabon Government." Rawlgeeb lowered the tablet and paused, his expression sour as a bulldog chewing a wasp. "You will be returned exactly to the point from which you were abducted, and that is to be an end to the matter. You're getting off lightly–very lightly indeed if you ask me–so you can keep your ridiculous wisecracks to yourself."

Brent frowned. "I'm going home? Are you serious?"

"Deadly." Rawlgeeb traced a pattern on the tablet with his fingertip. "I hereby release the sample reference HK796765, also identified as Brent Bolster, and initiate the process of return." He tucked the tablet under his arm and gestured toward the door. "Release the sample."

The guard on Rawlgeeb's right stepped forward, a small key held ready in his huge and meaty fist. Brent watched him fumble with the lock. *This is really happening*, he thought. *I'm out of here*. But he couldn't rejoice in his good fortune. "Wait. I don't buy it. Is this some kind of trick?"

"Certainly not," Rawlgeeb replied. "Unlikely as it seems, you apparently have friends in high places. Your membership of the AGI was reinstated and backdated. Apparently, your membership fees were paid by an anonymous benefactor, and he or she made representations to the Gloabon High

Command."

The guard finally mastered the lock and pulled the door open. Brent watched in silence. The squeak of the hinges was exactly as Brent had imagined it, but still, it felt too good to be true. He glanced back at Maisie. "She comes with me."

Rawlgeeb grunted. "Ridiculous. Each sample is treated separately, and the details of each person sampled are confidential. If she is to be returned, I will not, under any circumstances, discuss the matter with you. That would be unthinkable."

Brent stepped back, away from the open door. "I'm not kidding. Either she comes with me, or I stay, and we'll see what that does to your precious paperwork."

Rawlgeeb turned to the guard on his left. "It's been a while since I carried a sidearm, but tell me, does a parton pistol come with a stun setting these days."

"Oh yes," the guard said, drawing his weapon. "It's not automatic though. It's more of a manual setting, you might say." He turned his gun around, gripping it firmly by the barrel and pounding the weapon's sturdy grip against the palm of his other hand. He grinned, his lips curling to reveal two rows of crooked teeth. "A swift swipe to the back of the head usually does it. I know it's a bit predictable, but it's nice to keep the old traditions alive, that's what I always say." He stepped into the doorway, his broad shoulders barely fitting through the frame.

Brent held up his hands, his fingers spread wide. "Take it easy, big fella. You heard what your boss said. I'm meant to be going home, remember?"

"Yes," Rawlgeeb put in, "but I didn't say anything about you being in one piece. So if you'd rather not cooperate, then I'll have no option but to let my colleague experiment with his…what did call it? Ah, yes, his *manual setting*." He paused, looking thoughtful. "I just hope he doesn't have to hit you *too* many times before you lose consciousness. It's not easy getting the blood off this deck, and the cleaning crew is a long way behind on their schedule."

Maisie marched to Brent's side. "Brent, just go, for God's sake. Nobody asked you to stay on my account. I'm not a damsel in distress, and even if I were, you wouldn't exactly be my idea of a knight in shining armor."

"What?" Brent's eyes narrowed. "Of all the ungrateful…"

Maisie didn't give him a chance to finish. She shoved him with all her might, and Brent fell against the guard, forcing the huge alien to stagger back into the corridor and collide with the second guard. Rawlgeeb ducked back to avoid becoming entangled in their flailing limbs, and Maisie took her chance, racing through the open door and along the corridor, her long legs making short work of the distance. Recovering, one of the guards raised his pistol, but Brent charged into him, pushing the brute's arm upward. A ray of glittering light erupted from the weapon, slicing a neat gash in the ceiling, and a stream of thick smoke poured from the hole.

Somewhere, an alarm sounded, and the guards composed themselves, both taking aim at Brent's chest. "Let *me* do it," the first guard growled. "He owes me."

"Shit!" Brent turned to Rawlgeeb. "Call him off. I'm immune. I shouldn't be here. You signed the order to send me back, I saw you. If I don't turn up back on Earth, you'll be held liable."

"Flek!" Rawlgeeb muttered. "Stand down, you two. He's right."

Brent straightened his clothes. "Thank you for nothing. Now, send me home, and while you're about it, send the girl back too. Anyone can see she's more trouble than she's worth, and she works for the UN–she told me herself. She's supposed to be immune too, so she's only going to cause more problems for you further down the line. Believe me, I only met her five minutes ago, and she's driven me half-crazy already."

Rawlgeeb snorted, the thin slits of his nostrils flaring. "You really have absolutely no idea how this works." He turned to the guards. "I'll take care of this one, you two can go and get the female. She can't have gone far. Throw her back in a holding cell until I'm ready to process her, and this time put shackles on her. If she struggles, sedate her."

The guards set off at a trot, and Brent's anger flared. "Wait a goddamned minute!" He lunged forward, and when Rawlgeeb blocked his path, he didn't back down, but instead, he got up close and personal with the Gloabon, jabbing his finger hard in the alien's bony chest. "Don't you dare lay a finger on that girl! Didn't you hear what I said? She's with the UN. They'll have your head on a plate then feed it to what's left of the alligators."

"Oh, the UN," Rawlgeeb said. "That's different. Of course, we'll send her home immediately. We'll send flowers, take her out to dinner, and afterward, perhaps a show. Ha!" A harsh, braying erupted from his throat, and Brent winced. The sound of Gloabon laughter had always struck him as faintly irritating, but in close proximity, the grating croak of Rawlgeeb's guffaw set his teeth on edge.

"The UN!" Rawlgeeb leaned closer to Brent, adopting a conspiratorial tone. "The UN may make a fuss for a while. They might call up our Customer Services department or even file an official complaint, but in the end, they will do exactly what we tell them to do."

"No," Brent muttered, but when Rawlgeeb nodded with a knowing grin, Brent fell silent, his mind performing cartwheels. Was nothing sacred? The UN was supposed to be the last bastion of hope for the human race; could it really be in thrall to the Gloabon Government?

Rawlgeeb took Brent's arm, guiding him along the corridor. "Right, let's get you sent home. Some of us have got quotas to fill."

"But, what you said–that can't be right," Brent began, but Rawlgeeb cut him off by the simple act of producing the gleaming, metallic band from his pocket.

"Am I going to have to use the restrictor, or can we send you back the easy way?"

Brent stared at the silvery band, a shiver running up his spine as the details of his abduction came flooding back: the sensation of being frozen solid and then shattered, his body paralyzed as it was torn apart. He drew a shaky breath. "What's the easy way?"

"There's the zinger. It's a little slower than the zip but much more pleasant." He grinned. "It's what we use."

"How about a good, old-fashioned shuttle?"

"Alas, no," Rawlgeeb replied. "Shuttles are reserved for the High Command. But don't worry, I use the zinger all the time, and it hasn't done me any harm." When Rawlgeeb smiled, the left side of his face twitched erratically, but the alien didn't seem to notice.

"Right." Brent had no faith in the Gloabons' technology whatsoever. As far as he could see, the only devices they were good at constructing were weapons and automated rotisseries. In Brent's book, the Gloabon Government was defined by its twin cravings for galactic domination and perfectly roasted reptiles. But in this case, it looked as though he'd have to rely on their transportation to get home. What choice did he have? "So, what do I have to do? Do you have a special room or something?"

"Not necessary on this occasion. Just stand very still, and I'll take care of it." Rawlgeeb tapped on the screen of his tablet. "I'll just tag you and send your home address to the computer, and the system will take care of the rest. You won't feel a thing."

Brent rolled his shoulders, readying himself, staring straight ahead. *Home, here I come*, he thought. He could almost smell the extra strength fresh coffee he kept in the freezer. He'd tried keeping the tub of ground beans elsewhere, but the neighbors had complained. Now, he was ready for a brew so strong it would make his eyeballs spin, and if he didn't sleep for a week afterward, that was just fine. "Goodbye, Rawlplug, my old friend. It's been real. Any time you feel like stopping by for a chat, give me a call, and I'll make sure I'm out of town."

"Very droll," Rawlgeeb said. He tapped his screen once more, and as a faint tingling spread along Brent's arms, Rawlgeeb smiled unpleasantly. "Of course, when I said you wouldn't feel a thing, I was thinking of Gloabon physiology. For humans, I believe the sensation is quite different."

"Are you kidding me?" Brent protested, but it was too late to back down now. The tingling was already growing stronger, spreading across his back, raking across his skin like the touch an inexperienced and yet over-enthusiastic masseur.

"I'm told that it's a little like being slapped across the face."

Brent almost laughed. "That's not so bad. Happens to me all the time."

But Rawlgeeb hadn't finished. "While at the same time, being turned inside out."

"You bastard!" Brent spluttered. But although he had plenty more to say, he was unable to form a coherent sentence; he was too busy screaming.

CHAPTER 8

Gloabon Space Station *The Gamulon* - Earth Orbit

Rawlgeeb pressed the call button on the door to Breamell's quarters, and as he waited, he plucked a fleck of dust from the lapel of his best tunic, fingers trembling. *What am I doing here? She won't want to be seen with someone like me.* He glanced along the empty corridor. No one had seen him arrive. If he walked away now, no one would know, and he could send Breamell a message giving her some excuse or other. *Don't be such a coward*, he chided himself. *Grow a trio.* It was too late anyhow. He could hear movement from beyond the door. He stiffened his spine and tried to look relaxed, but he had a terrible suspicion that instead of a suave smile, he was grinning like a witless buffoon.

The door slid open with a gentle hiss, and when Breamell stepped toward him, Rawlgeeb could only stand and stare. Something in his chest was clearly malfunctioning, and he wondered for a split second whether he might need medical attention. He'd heard the expression *heart-melting*, but he'd never realized that it could be taken quite so literally. Breamell was utterly captivating, her skin glistening with a lustrous sheen, her eyes shining, her dazzling smile showing her perfectly pointed ivory teeth. Rawlgeeb's mind reeled, and though he'd prepared exactly what he'd been going to say, when he opened his mouth, his vocabulary shrank to only three words, none of which were appropriate.

Breamell's smile faded. "Rawlgeeb, are you all right? Are you ill?"

"No, no. I was just, er...never mind. You look nice. Very nice. Very, very nice. Your jumpsuit is most, er, it is also very nice."

"Do you like it?" Breamell turned around, and Rawlgeeb could not help but goggle at the way the lustrous fabric clung tightly to her trim figure. "I made it myself. It's not too informal, is it? Only with your colleagues being there, I wanted to make a good impression."

Rawlgeeb's heart sank when he remembered they were meeting Clactonbury and Pentledaw. The pair would probably try to muscle in on his date, monopolizing the conversation with their foolish jokes. But maybe he'd have an opportunity to ditch them and have Breamell all to himself. They could find somewhere quiet and stroll along together, arm in arm, talking of their hopes and dreams. And then later, perhaps he might steal a kiss, their lips meeting, her eyes growing wide in the moonlight.

"Seriously, are you sure you're all right?" Breamell asked. "You really don't look well."

Rawlgeeb ran his hand over his brow and managed a smile. "I'm fine. Absolutely fine. We should get going. Are you happy for me to use my zinger?"

"Of course." She stepped to his side, and when he pulled his handset from his pocket, she let out an appreciative murmur. "The latest model. They must certainly be paying you well in liaison."

"You know, I'm out and about a lot. It's important that I keep in touch." Feeling a surge of confidence, he offered her his hand. "Here, if you haven't done this very often, it makes the trip more comfortable if we hold onto one another."

She grasped his hand firmly, her eyes glistening with excitement. "I haven't zinged for ages. The last time I tried it, I felt a bit ill, but I'm sure I'll be fine, especially with you by my side."

Rawlgeeb's internal organs now made up for having let

him down earlier, rallying around and pulling themselves together, carrying out their tasks with newfound enthusiasm. If someone had asked him to perform backflips along the corridor, he'd have given it a damned good go. Perhaps fortunately, at least for the sake of his best suit, all that was required of him was the pressing of a single icon on his handset, and as the zinger sent its electromagnetic tendrils to encase their bodies, he scarcely felt a thing.

**

Rawlgeeb had visited the arrivals lounge on Earth so many times that he scarcely saw it in detail anymore; it was a port of call, a stopping off point in his every working day. But when he arrived with Breamell, she turned around on the spot, her expression a picture of delight and amazement. "The lights," she breathed. "The windows, the…what are those floppy green things?"

Rawlgeeb was puzzled for a second until he realized what she was pointing at. "Those are potted plants," he said knowledgeably. "Palms mainly. It's a human thing. They pull them up and bring them indoors, and then they bring them water and so on to keep them alive."

"To eat?" Breamell asked.

"No. It's more, just for the sake of it. They often choose species that are quite likely to die. Those over there, for example, are from countries with much hotter climates. It's odd really." He shrugged. "You know how it is. Humans like to keep themselves busy. It gives them something to do."

Breamell giggled. "I don't think I'll ever understand them."

"Probably better that way," Rawlgeeb said. "Shall we

find somewhere to wait? My colleagues should be with us soon. There's a bar. We could have a drink while we wait."

"Yes please." Breamell was practically dancing on the spot. "That sounds perfect."

"This way." Rawlgeeb gestured across the room, and as they walked, he almost jumped when she took his arm. It was as though his earlier daydream was becoming a reality in front of his eyes. He had the urge to pinch himself.

"Hey, Rawlgeeb! Over here!"

Rawlgeeb snapped out of his trance without the need for a physical stimulus; his coworkers were doing the job just fine. Clactonbury was waving to him from the executive bar, and perched on a stool by his side, Pentledaw was staring at Breamell lasciviously.

I should've known, he thought. *It was too good to last.* But when he looked down at Breamell and bathed in her smile, his mood quickly recovered. "It looks as though my colleagues are here already. Are you happy to go and meet them?"

"Of course. That's why we came here in the first place, wasn't it?"

"Yes," Rawlgeeb replied. "Yes, it was. But maybe later…"

"Come on," Breamell said, tugging at his arm. "Let's network."

Rawlgeeb couldn't quite keep the disappointment out of his tone. "All right. I suppose that's why you agreed to come along, after all."

Breamell pursed her lips. "Only indirectly." She smiled up at him and spoke quietly so that only he could hear. "I'm here to support you, Rawlgeeb. Don't take this the wrong way, but I thought you might need a little help–socially, I mean. And I wanted to help you because, not to put too fine a point on it, I think you're rather nice."

"Oh," Rawlgeeb said, and though the word was entirely inadequate, he hoped his smile might make up for it.

"So let's get on with it," Breamell went on. "And then later...we'll take it from there. Okay?"

Rawlgeeb nodded vigorously. "More than okay. Absolutely perfect." And with Breamell clinging tightly to his arm, they strode into the executive bar together.

***

"But don't you see?" Rawlgeeb asked, waving his hands in the air with such enthusiasm that his third martini slopped over the rim of his glass. "That's what makes liaison so interesting!"

"If you say so," Clactonbury drawled. "I know it's not politically correct and all, but after a while, the humans all start to look the same to me."

"No, no, no," Rawlgeeb retorted. He took a slurp of his drink. "It's all the little things–the foibles, the quirks that make them so fascinating." He gestured across the executive bar. "Take those for example. Cheese plants. Why?"

"Who cares?" Pentledaw said. "When you get down to it, I'm not sure why humans do anything. Most of what they do just seems like a tremendous waste of time to me."

"Ha!" Rawlgeeb pointed his finger at Pentledaw. "That's my point exactly! No other species in the galaxy is so wonderfully, so magnificently, so elaborately *trivial!* They're unique."

Clactonbury and Pentledaw exchanged a look, and Breamell laid her hand gently on Rawlgeeb's arm. "I think you've made your point. Maybe we should get some fresh air. You were going to show me around, remember?"

"In a minute," Rawlgeeb said, patting her hand. "We should just get one more drink while we put the world to rights." He chortled. "The world, get it? *This* world. We're putting it right, aren't we? Upgrading it, little by little."

"I think you've had enough," Clactonbury said gruffly. "I guess you're not used to Earth liquor."

"Oh, I don't know," Pentledaw said quickly. "Our friend is just letting off a little steam, that's all. You know what? I think I know just what he might like." He waved to attract the barman's attention, and when the human bartender marched briskly across to take his order, Pentledaw said, "Do you have the makings of a black Russian by any chance?"

The barman pursed his lips, his expert eye assessing his customers. He seemed particularly interested in Rawlgeeb who was swaying slightly as he drained his glass. "Sir, we are fully stocked with a wide range of beverages from Earth and from across the galaxy. However, if the drink is for you and your friends, I have to advise you that Kahlua is made from–"

"Yes, yes," Pentledaw interrupted. "We know all that. We're all adults here. Just give us a black Russian, two more martinis, and…" He looked at Breamell. "Are you sure you won't join us in an Earth drink, my dear? You've been sipping that swamp sap special for a long time."

"I like it," Breamell replied. "It reminds me of home. We used to make it ourselves back on Gloabon."

Clactonbury flashed her a wolfish smile. "Maybe, but when in Rome…"

"All right then," Breamell said. "What do you think I'd like?"

"Tequila," Clactonbury stated. "It's made from a desert plant, and I think you'll enjoy its subtle flavor. It's very much a traditional Earth thing. You lick the salt, gulp down the drink in one, then suck on a chunk of green fruit. Personally, I'd avoid the last part if I were you. One day last week, Pentledaw and me had eight or ten tequilas and afterward my stomach was on fire. And what was worse, the next morning my head damned near split in two. I almost shed my skin. I blame all that fruit–way too much citric acid."

Breamell hesitated, but there was a gleam in her eye. "Go on then. Just one."

"Coming up, sir." The barman's hands were already busy. "Here's your black Russian, but I really must–"

"Thank you," Pentledaw said quickly, slapping his credit card on the counter. "And don't forget to take a generous tip for yourself."

The barman scooped up the card. "Thank you, sir. Enjoy your drinks." He processed the card quickly then returned it with a flourish before scooting away.

"Now," Pentledaw said, handing the glass of dark liquid to Rawlgeeb, "I think you're going to *love* this."

Rawlgeeb beamed, all his earlier worries taking flight. How silly he'd been; worrying about nothing. Here he was on Earth, enjoying a sophisticated local beverage with his new best friends. And to top it all, he had a beautiful young companion at his side. Everything was for the best. Everything was exactly as it should be. And from this point on, things would only get better. "Thank you," he said, raising his glass in the way that humans did. "Here's to us." A fragment of something he'd read somewhere popped into his mind, and he added, "Confusion to the enemy!"

"Confusion to the enemy!" his friends chorused, and

since Breamell was finishing her drink in one gulp, Rawlgeeb followed her lead, draining the strange flavored drink in one mouthful.

"Hell's teeth!" Rawlgeeb hissed. "That was *good!* So *damned good!*" He licked his lips, his eyes alight with feverish desire. "I have to have another. Bartender! Bartender, over here! *Quick!*"

"Er, hold on, buddy," Clactonbury said gently, but Rawlgeeb pushed past him.

Rawlgeeb pounded the bar with his fist. "Come on! Let's get some service over here. In fact, flek it, I'll get the damned drink myself." With a whoop, Rawlgeeb hoisted himself onto the bar and stood atop it, upsetting a row of drinks. He let out a wild yell and spun around, spreading his arms wide and cackling like a hyena, apparently forgetting his original intention.

Pentledaw collapsed in helpless laughter, but the party of Gloabon security guards standing next to him weren't so amused; Rawlgeeb had just knocked over their drinks, and two of them rounded on Pentledaw, giving him a shove. Pentledaw staggered back, and Clactonbury went to his friend's aide, glaring at the guards and raising his voice. Meanwhile, the barman was bravely trying to push Rawlgeeb down from the bar; no mean feat since Rawlgeeb was dodging and kicking out, darting from side to side as if dancing to a frenetic beat that only he could hear.

"I can fly!" Rawlgeeb crowed, hopping from one foot to the other, his arms thrashing wildly in all directions. "I can soar through the air!"

Breamell managed to grab hold of one of Rawlgeeb's legs, but when she pulled him back, she only succeeded in toppling him, and he landed heavily on the bar, scattering everything in a shower of glass, peanuts, and overpriced liquids.

The throng of customers let out a collective roar of anger.

Afterward, nobody could agree who'd thrown the first punch. But there was one thing on which everyone could agree: it had all been Rawlgeeb's fault.

CHAPTER 9

Earth

Brent opened his office door and shouldered his way inside, both door and owner emitting juddering groans as they completed their reluctant interaction. Brent clutched his head as he looked around the room, trying to make sense of what should've been familiar surroundings. But the place seemed odd as if everything in the room had been shifted around. Perhaps someone had turned the place over. *An unhappy client?* he wondered. *But which one? There've been so many.* He rubbed his temples, trying to prevent them from throbbing quite so loudly. His head felt as though his brain had been turning somersaults, and his memories were muddled and disjointed. He knew nothing of the last few days, but although his older recollections were a little hazy, they seemed relatively stable. He knew, for instance, that this was his place of work, and he remembered that at one time he'd had plenty of satisfied customers. He'd been good at his job. There'd been smiles and handshakes in this office; people had left with their hearts a little lighter, their eyes moist with tears of gratitude. Clients had sauntered back to their regular lives, pausing only to offer generous gratuities. But not anymore. Not since…

What was that? A muffled voice was coming from beyond the side door; a man's voice. *The intruder! He's still here!* Brent squared his shoulders. Whoever came through that door, they'd get what was coming to them. What the hell did they think they were doing, barging into his office and rifling through his belongings? How dare they?

The side door swung open, and Brent raised his fists. *That's right, buddy! Come and get what's owing to you!*

But the man who stepped into the room was a full head

taller than Brent and built like a brick outhouse, his shoulders almost filling the doorway. The guy had his back to Brent, and he was looking down as if intent on carrying something. Brent stared. Once again, he had the unsettling notion that this scene was strangely familiar, but he couldn't make sense of it. Brent kept his fists raised, but his hard expression was starting slip, and if he was honest, he was in no shape for a fist fight; he wouldn't have laid money on himself in an arm wrestle with an eighth-grader.

The intruder turned, humming a jaunty melody, and when he saw Brent, his broad, handsome face lit with a movie-star grin. "Boss! What are you doing here? It's only eleven." He let out a guffaw of hearty laughter. "Hell, I don't think I've ever seen you in the mornings before. I guess there's a first time for everything!"

Brent lowered his fists, sweat breaking out on his brow. So that was it. That was why the office looked so strange; he wasn't used to the morning sunlight pouring in through the grime-streaked windows. *Ugh!* He shook his head, the motion doing nothing for the pain swimming behind his eyes.

The tall man nodded toward the tray he was carrying. "I just brewed a pot of coffee. Want some?"

Brent's mind seized on the notion. *A cup of coffee.* That was the best idea he'd ever heard in his entire life. A slew of witty, one-line replies fought for his attention, tumbling over each other like excited puppies, but his mouth was so dry he could barely speak, and he settled for the minimum viable reply: "Yes. Coffee. Good."

"Sit down," the man said. "I'll fetch a mug." He set the tray down on a desk, but as he made to move away, Brent staggered forward and seized the steaming mug of coffee, lifting it to his lips with shaking hands and gulping half of it down in one go, letting the scalding liquid scorch his throat as it passed.

"Or you could just drink mine," the man added. "I guess I'll fix myself another." The man marched from the room, and Brent took stock. *There's something wrong with me*, he decided. *Also, there's a strange man in my office.* The man seemed to know him, but he couldn't recall the guy's name no matter how hard he tried. He felt like hell, and he had no idea why that should be. He only knew that, for some reason, he'd felt a strange compulsion to leave his apartment and stagger into the office. He'd woken up with a headache from hell, pulled on some clothes and hit the street, but all the while he'd felt oddly out of control. There was only one logical conclusion: he must've been on a bender. And judging by the tremors tingling his fingers, it must've lasted some considerable time.

The man strolled back in bearing a mug, and he made for the desk, scooping up something brown from a plate on the tray. "At least you didn't eat my doughnut. Guess I should be thankful for small mercies." He took a bite, chewing as he looked Brent up and down. "Seriously, boss, sit down before you fall down. You look like hell."

"In a second," Brent said. "Who, er, who are you...exactly?"

The man raised his eyebrows. "Vince. You know that. I work here."

"You do?"

Vince sighed. "Yes. I'm your assistant. Speaking of which, we need to talk about my salary. And when I say *talk about*, what I mean is, you need to give me the money. Preferably in cash. Today."

Brent clicked his fingers. "Now I remember. Vince. Vince Claybourne. Of course." He crossed to his desk and sat down carefully as if frightened the chair might collapse. The room was snapping into sharper focus now, and Brent cast his eyes over it. *What a shit hole*, he decided. *No wonder I can't face it in the mornings*. He turned his gaze on Vince. "Didn't I fire you?"

"Not recently."

"Okay. Good." Brent smiled. "You're fired. Now get the hell out of here."

Vince's shoulders slumped. "Here we go again. Same old routine." He sat back in his chair. "Finish your coffee, boss, and I'll get you another. Then we might get something like sense out of you, and you can tell me where you've been for the last ten days."

Brent froze. "Ten days? I was on a bender for ten days?"

"A bender?" Vince shook his head slowly, maintaining eye contact with Brent all the while. "Boss, you don't drink. Not for a long time. Not since…" He let his voice trail away, a sudden sadness in his eyes. "Listen, I don't know what you've got going on, but I'm pretty sure you haven't been hitting the bars. I'd have smelt it on you, and drugs have never been your thing, so whatever the problem is, it must be something different, like you've been sick or something. Is that it?"

Brent blinked, and while his addled consciousness played catch-up, he downed the rest of the coffee, feeling the caffeine scurrying into his veins, his heart racing.

"I tried calling you, but you never picked up," Vince went on. "I even stopped by your apartment a couple times, but no one answered. I figured you were working a case. I thought it was strange you hadn't left a note of the client's name or anything, because that's the one thing you usually remember, but there was nothing on your desk–nothing I could understand anyhow."

"Wait a second," Brent said, waving the empty mug in the air. "Did you say something about another cup of coffee?"

Vince heaved his hefty frame from his chair and crossed to Brent's desk where he stood, towering over his employer, his arms folded. "Just once, a please would be nice."

"Just get the damned coffee," Brent replied. "This isn't a goddamned finishing school for fuck's sake."

"And he's back." Vince plucked the empty mug from Brent's fingers and stalked from the room.

He's right, Brent decided. *I am starting to feel more like myself.* He let out a grunt. It was just a shame that he was obviously such an asshole. He cracked his knuckles and studied the contents of his desk. It looked as though someone, probably Vince, had tried to assert some kind of order on the stacks of paper. One pile consisted entirely of unpaid bills and final demands, another was made up of menus, mainly for Mexican food, but the third looked more interesting. The papers were crumpled and curling at the corners as if they'd been well-thumbed, and each sheet held news stories, printed out from online sources. Someone had spent hours poring over the stories, highlighting sentences in various bright colors, scribbling notes in the margins, circling key words. "I must've done this," Brent murmured. "I must be a pretty good investigator. Very thorough."

"Here you go." Vince marched back in and put the mug down on the desk.

"Thanks," Brent said absently. He looked up. "So, this is what I was working on? Something to do with the Gloabons?"

Vince's face fell. "Ah, those are mine. Something I've

been putting together." He snatched up the pile of papers. "I was using your desk. Sorry. I didn't mean to leave my stuff there."

"Oh." Brent took a sip of coffee. "Right. So what was *I* doing? I mean, if I've been gone for ten days, I must've been doing *something*."

"No idea. It's not like you let me in on every little thing you do." Vince returned to his own desk and stashed the papers in a drawer. "You know, I could do a lot more to help around here if you gave me the chance. I'm working on getting my license, but they'll never let me into the AGI if I don't have some kind of experience."

Brent sat bolt upright, his head startlingly clear. "The AGI. That's it!" He fumbled in his pocket and pulled out his wallet, opening it with trembling fingers. His AGI card was there, and he held it close, studying the tiny rows of neat lettering arranged across its surface. The card's chip was linked to the net via an encrypted channel, and its details could be updated automatically. His membership had lapsed, he was sure of that, but now it had been renewed and extended for a full ten years. And more than that, his membership status had been changed. "I got an upgrade," he whispered. "Platinum. I'm a goddamned platinum member of the AGI."

Vince was out of his chair. "What?"

Brent showed him the card. "See for yourself."

"Holy hell. Whatever you've been doing, it must've been pretty damned important. They don't just give those things out for nothing."

Brent rubbed his chin, his nails catching on his thick stubble. "Either that or somebody wants something from me. Somebody wants me on a leash, and this is the way to get me there."

"Who? There aren't many people with that kind of clout–not in this town. Not anymore. Hell, there aren't many people on the planet who can pull those strings."

"Exactly," Brent said, jabbing his finger at a piece of paper on his desk. "And that's what makes this item here very important."

Vince's brow furrowed. "That flyer? How is that significant?"

"Because it tells me that the lunchtime special is half price down at Martha's, and that in turn leads me to the highly relevant fact that I'm incredibly hungry." He stood quickly, almost toppling his chair. "Now, if you were a platinum level investigator like me, you'd realize that I can't possibly solve a case this complex when I'm half-starved, so I'm heading out for lunch, and I may be some time."

"Shall I come with you? Maybe we could even figure out a few leads over lunch."

Brent eyed him suspiciously. "That depends. Do you have money?"

Vince nodded enthusiastically. "Plenty."

"Then you're coming. Also, as an important step in your learning process, you'll be picking up the tab." He tapped the side of his nose. "It's how these things work. A central plank of the investigators' code is this: never pay for your own lunch. Have you got that? Maybe you should write it down."

"Believe me," Vince said, "I learned that lesson a long time ago."

"Good. Well done. There's hope for you yet. Never let the details slip. Grab hold of every tiny detail and hold it tight. You never know when something might turn out to be important. Right, lead the way."

They made for the door, but Brent suddenly doubled back and grabbed the flyer from his desk. "Almost forgot. I'm not entirely sure where Martha's actually is. The address is right here." He tucked the flyer into his pocket, and this time, he made it out the door without incident.

***

The owner of Martha's Place had clearly given an interior decorator free reign, and as Brent scanned the room, searching for a vacant table, he felt his high hopes sinking in the pit of his empty stomach. *This joint is too busy trying to be different*, he told himself, *same as every other goddamned place*. He strolled toward the counter, the heels of his shoes catching on the uneven floorboards, and Vince followed close behind.

"I guess they really went for that Industrial Age chic," Vince said, admiring a gleaming wall. "The last time I saw this much sheet steel was on one of those history shows on TV."

Brent's only reply was a grunt, but when he reached the counter, he tapped its surface with his knuckle. "Fake. Synthetic. Not even real plastic. I doubt whether there's a single ounce of solid steel in the whole place."

"Oh." Vince's smile vanished, and Brent studied the young man with something approaching pity; the kid really needed to get wise to the ways of the world. He needed toughening up, teaching a lesson or two. And maybe this mystery of the missing ten days, whatever the cause turned out to be, might be just the opportunity to set the kid on the right track. He could let him tag along for a while. After all,

Vince might be soft, but he had a physique that would intimidate most people. Sometimes a big guy could provide a little leverage just by showing up, and according to Brent's first rule of physics, a little leverage could go a long way. *Just so long as I can get the kid to keep his trap shut*, he thought.

A young man wearing bright blue overalls and a hard hat appeared on the other side of the counter and greeted them with a grin. His name badge read *Matt* and proclaimed his title as *Food Engineer First Class*. "Welcome to Martha's. Table for two? Would you like to see a menu first?"

Brent looked along the row of tall stools drawn up to the counter. "Can't we just eat here?"

Matt bowed his head. "Sorry, sir. They're just for show. But we can find you a table, no problem at all."

Brent pulled at a stool and found that it was bolted to the floor, the seat disappearing beneath the counter's edge so that the stool couldn't be used with any comfort.

"A table for two would be fine," Vince said. "Anywhere is just great."

"No, we need somewhere quiet," Brent put in. "We have business to discuss."

"Sure." Matt waved to a young woman who seemed to be dressed as a production line worker, complete with plastic safety spectacles and orange ear defenders. Daubs of something like grime had been artfully daubed on her cheeks.

"This way," she yelled. "Follow me." She set off across the restaurant, and Brent followed, his hands in his pockets. The woman pointed to a table, shouting, "Here's your table. I'll be back to take your order in a minute. Can I get you something to drink?"

"Coffee," Brent said, opening his mouth wide to enunciate the word as clearly as he could, but the woman just frowned. "Coffee!" Brent called. "Why don't you take those damned things off your ears?"

The woman put her hands on her hips. "Do you want a drink or not?"

"Let me," Vince said, putting his hands together to form a letter *T*.

Realization dawned on the woman's face. "Two teas coming up," she said and hurried away.

"I don't want tea," Brent complained. "What am I, your maiden aunt?"

"All right, wiseguy," Vince said, taking a seat, "you tell me how to mime the word *coffee*."

Brent sat heavily, casting a glance at the table of six people right next to them. Almost certainly a family group, they were all vying for the title of Loudest Person in the Room, their conversation limited to whatever boxset they were currently obsessed by. They had strong opinions on the lead actors, who were either brilliant or completely inept depending on whether you listened to the shiny-faced youngsters or the jaded older members of the group, the latter looking as though they'd given up caring about most things a long time ago. But whatever their stance, all members of the group were unwilling to give way on any point, no matter how insignificant.

"I can hardly hear myself think," Brent said. "I asked for somewhere quiet."

Vince shrugged. "I guess it is, as far as our waitress is concerned. I'm starting to see why she wears the ear defenders. I wonder if she could let me have a pair."

"Never mind that. We need to start work. I have ten days

to piece together, so why don't we start with the last time you saw me."

"Let me see," Vince began. "Wait, here come our drinks."

The waitress placed two mugs on the table. "Are you ready to order?"

Vince started a complex series of gestures, but Brent waved his attempt aside, then he pulled the flyer from his pocket. He pointed at the special offer, making sure his finger was on exactly the right place, then he pointed at Vince and himself.

The waitress leaned forward to study the flyer, then she cast him a dismissive look. "It's Thursday."

Brent frowned, baffled. He fought the urge to pluck the ear defenders from the girl and settled instead for an exaggerated Gallic shrug.

"You can have two bowls of the special chili," the girl intoned, "but they're only half price on Wednesdays between eleven and eleven forty-five. So you can either pay full price or come back next week."

"Next week! What the hell are you talking about?" Brent slapped the flyer down on the table, pointing repeatedly to the correct item. "I don't care," he yelled. "Just give us the goddamned chili. One each. Today. Not next week. Now!"

"Fine," the waitress said. "No need to be like that." She flounced away, and Brent realized that the family on the next table had fallen silent, all of them regarding him with profound distaste. "Really," the matriarch of the group grumbled. "Some people!"

Brent leaned his elbows on the table and held his head in hands. "This day had better not get any worse, or I swear I'll do something I regret."

"Let's get started on the case," Vince said hopefully. "The last time I heard from you was on a Sunday. I called you up at around five o'clock to remind you about paying me, and you promised faithfully to do it the very next day."

Brent narrowed his eyes. "Really? That doesn't sound like the kind of thing I'd say."

"All right, I made that last part up, but you can't blame a fella for trying." Vince grinned. "The first part was true though. I called you, and you told me I'd get paid but I'd have to stand in line and wait my turn."

"Then what?"

"Then you hung up. I won't lie to you—we've had that same conversation plenty of times, and that's pretty much the way it always goes."

Brent sat back. Every word had the ring of truth, and though he hated to admit it, the more he remembered about himself, the less he liked what he heard. "So, why do you stay? A young guy like you, you must be able to get a better job."

"Like I said back in the office, I want my investigator's license, and you took me on." He thought for a moment. "I'll level with you since you seem to have forgotten pretty much everything. I don't have any qualifications, and I don't have any references, but I do have a conviction for hacking into a computer system, and that's always counted against me. But when I told you about it, you weren't concerned. In fact, you seemed quite interested."

"Who did you hack? A bank? A secret government database?" Brent smirked then took a sip of tea.

"No. It was stupid really." Vince drew circles on the table with his finger, then he lowered his voice and said, "I hijacked a UN drone and sent it circling around my buddies' houses just for kicks. But I got caught, you know, by the Gloabons."

"Holy shit!" Brent cried out. One of the children on the next table goggled at him, but Brent took no notice. "Something's coming back to me."

"Is it something about the Gloabons? Did they have something to do with your disappearance? I mean, they can't have abducted you because of your immunity, but–"

Brent grabbed Vince's arm, pressing it hard against the table. "No. It's more important than that. I've remembered that if there's one thing I really can't stand, it's tea." He pointed accusingly at the mug. "Especially goddamned English Breakfast. Agh! Disgusting!"

The waitress sidled up to the table bearing two bowls of chili and plonked them down on the table without ceremony. "I hope she's not expecting a tip," Brent murmured, and the young woman shot him a hostile look. Some phrases, it seemed, passed straight through her ear defenders without hindrance.

"Thank you," Vince yelled. "This looks delicious."

"Enjoy," she replied without enthusiasm then strolled away, oblivious to the many diners who called out to her as she passed.

Brent grabbed a fork and tucked into his chili. "This ain't bad." He chewed thoughtfully. "Mediocre, definitely, but bad would be an overstatement." He swallowed and took another forkful. "Okay, we talked on a Sunday at five. When did you next try calling me?"

"The next day, around noon," Vince replied. "No answer. I tried three or four times, but you never picked up. Then over the next week and a half, I called once a day, but there was never any answer."

"Ten days—I still can't get over it." Brent laid down his fork. "Are you sure I don't drink? Because I'm telling you, I could use a stiff one right about now."

"Definitely. I haven't seen you take anything stronger than coffee for a long time. You swore not to touch a drop when…" he hesitated. "You must remember what happened, surely. I don't know if I can go over it now." He glanced at the neighboring table. "Not here."

Brent shook his head. "I'm drawing a blank on that. But I remember something though."

"Don't tell me you don't like chili because I *know* that isn't true."

"No. I remember *her*."

Vince followed Brent's gaze, and together they watched a tall, smartly dressed woman saunter across the restaurant. "You wish," Vince muttered. "Forget it, Brent, she wouldn't look at you twice. And she's definitely not one of your clients. There's no way I would've forgotten her."

"I'm serious," Brent insisted. "I know her." He raised his hand to point at her, and when she turned and saw him, Brent was one hundred percent certain. "Her name is Maisie. Maisie Richmond."

For a full second, Maisie and Brent stared at each other, and Vince looked from one to the other, his head swiveling like a plastic dog on a parcel shelf.

"What is she, an actress?" Vince asked. "You must've seen her on TV or something."

"Don't you get it?" Brent demanded. "She knows what happened to me. She knows because she was *there*." He stood clumsily, squeezing out from behind the table, and at the same time, Maisie turned away and started walking, heading for the exit with long strides. "Come on, Vince! We have to catch her." Brent set off in pursuit, but the waitress blocked his path, waving a check in the air.

Brent pointed at Vince who was shoveling forkfuls of chili into his mouth as he stood. "He's paying." Brent rubbed his forefinger and thumb together then pointed at Vince.

"Excuse me," Vince was saying as he picked his way between the tables, his bulky frame proving a disadvantage. "Excuse me. Oops! Sorry about that. Don't worry, that'll wash right out."

"For God's sake!" Brent snatched the check from the young woman's fingers and passed it back to Vince. "Him. Chase him. And get the hell out of my way." The waitress caught sight of the chaos Vince was causing, and Brent took advantage of her confusion, side-stepping neatly around her and making for the door. Maisie had beaten him to it, but the door was still swinging, and Brent barged through.

Out on the sidewalk, Maisie had taken off in earnest, running at a good speed despite her high heels and pencil skirt. She looked over her shoulder then increased her pace, and Brent went after her. "Maisie! Wait!" he called out, but if she heard him, she did not respond other than to dart into a side-street.

Brent slowed to a jog. His memories of the city might be impaired, but his intuition was still sharp, and something told him that his quarry had taken refuge in a dead-end street. He had her cornered.

"Boss! Wait up." Vince pounded along the sidewalk to join him. "What happened? Did you lose her?"

Brent pointed. "She ducked into that alley, but we'd better be careful."

"You think it's a trap?" Vince's eyes were round with

awe. "Did someone send her to find you, so she could lure you to your doom?"

"Seriously?" Brent ran his hand through his hair. "Where did you get that idea—some stupid true crime magazine?"

"Of course not. It stands to reason, that's all. It fits."

"Vince, whatever this is, it's probably not going to be a thrilling, glamorous conspiracy, all right? I'll bet there are a thousand explanations for what's going on, and every single one of them will be as dull as a drizzly Sunday in Des Moines."

"Hey, my Aunt Bethany lives in Des Moines."

Brent folded his arms "No doubt she's a case in point, but we're getting sidetracked. Back in the real world, if we go haring into a dead-end alley after a girl, she might just figure on fighting her way out. For all we know, she might be carrying a weapon."

"Or she might've called the cops," Vince put in.

"Now you're thinking," Brent said. "Either way, we could end up in trouble."

"Let me put it another way, boss. I think she called the cops. Look." Vince's eyes went to something behind Brent's shoulder, and as Brent turned around, a police cruiser glided to a halt just a few feet away.

"Let's take a walk," Brent said smoothly. "Just a couple of guys out for a stroll."

"Police! Hold it right there, sir."

"What do we do?" Vince hissed. "Do we run?"

Brent sighed. "We comply with the nice officers. We remember that we didn't do anything wrong, and we definitely don't mention anything about chasing after mysterious ladies. All right?"

"Got it."

The pair of police officers strode toward them, standard issue mirror shades hiding their eyes. "What's the hurry?" one of them demanded.

"No hurry," Brent said. "Just eager to get back to work, that's all."

The second officer held out his hand. "ID."

Brent and Vince produced their wallets, and the officers scrutinized their drivers' licenses, recording the details with their handheld scanners before passing them back.

Brent smiled throughout the process, but his beatific expression faltered when Maisie appeared at the alley's mouth.

"Excuse me, officers," she said. "I was the one who called you." She held out an ID of her own, and the officers stood tall, making a full assessment of her appearance before they glanced at her credentials.

"Thank you, ma'am. Are these the men who were harassing you?"

Maisie held eye contact with Brent, and a flicker of mischief lit her eyes. She was enjoying the moment, and she wanted him to know it.

"Harassing?" Brent asked. "Goodness me, what a terrible thing to suggest. I've never seen this woman before in my life. Unless…" He looked skyward as if deep in thought. "Wait a moment though. Did we meet at the fundraiser? Let's see…alligators wasn't it? You were there on behalf of the UN."

"Perhaps," Maisie said. "You have a remarkably good memory, Mr…"

"Bolster, but please call me Brent." He held out his hand. "A pleasure to meet you again, Ms. Richmond."

"Likewise. I'm sorry if I've caused you some trouble, Brent. A couple of uncouth hoodlums were pursuing me. Awful, criminal types. They had a deranged look. Deadbeats. Drug addicts probably. Or worse."

"Really? Are you sure?" Brent asked with a rictus grin. "Perhaps they were innocent guys who merely wanted to ask a few simple questions?"

Maisie grimaced. "Definitely not. These were villains. You know the kind. Vermin. Scum. The dregs of society."

The police officers were watching this charade with undisguised suspicion, but the tense silence was broken by a bleep from the radios the officers wore on their vests. One of the officers pressed a finger against his set, and after a brief hiss, a faint message came through. Brent couldn't make it all out, but he caught his name and a phrase that sounded like, "do not detain him in any way."

"All right, you're good to go, Mr. Bolster," the cop said. "Looks like you have friends in all the right places."

"Always nice to have friends," Brent replied without dropping his broad smile, but something in the police officer's phrase had tugged at his memory, plucking at a tight knot in the tangle of his battered consciousness. *Friends in high places.* The words ran through his mind like street urchins on the run, kicking over his cerebral furniture and upsetting cartloads of mental images into the bargain.

The officers turned their attention to Maisie. "Miss Richmond, do you need a ride? We can swing past the UN and drop you right by the door. No trouble at all."

"Why thank you," Maisie said. "That would be wonderful. How kind of you. That's exactly where I was headed next."

Both officers smiled, and one said, "Always a pleasure

to help the good folks up at the UN."

"Yeah, I must be getting back to work too," Brent chipped in. "My office is on Ganymede Street, not far from here. So my associate and I will walk."

"Whatever," one of the cops said as he climbed into the cruiser.

His colleague held the door open for Maisie then shut it firmly before climbing inside himself. The cop looked out through the open side window, and as the car pulled back into the traffic, he stared at Brent for a lot longer than was necessary.

"That woman," Brent murmured, "is nothing but trouble." But deep down he knew that if he was ever going to find out what had happened to him, Maisie Richmond was going to play a very important part.

CHAPTER 10

Gloabon Space Station *The Gamulon* - Earth Orbit

Rawlgeeb paced across his cell. *Ten days*, he thought. *Ten days in this stinking hellhole, and all because Pentledaw gave me that damned drink!* He thumped his fist against the wall. It could've been a wonderful night. Perfect. He could've impressed his superiors and won the affection of Breamell, but instead, it had all ended in disaster. "I never even made it out of the executive lounge," he whispered. "And now I'm finished. Done for."

Footsteps boomed in the corridor outside and Rawlgeeb braced himself, ready to face whatever humiliation was about to arrive. The guards had not taken kindly to seeing one of their own in the cells, and they'd taken every opportunity to make their feelings plain. A short while ago, Rawlgeeb would've agreed with them. He'd have said that high-ranking administrators who threw their privileges aside and misbehaved, had no one but themselves to blame. And if someone just happened to put gobbets of slime in the prisoners' food or woke them in the middle of the night with a few carefully aimed strokes of the sonic lash, then the miscreants were only getting what they deserved.

Now though, Rawlgeeb made a silent pledge to be kinder to all those who'd been punished in the past. It was all too easy to make a mistake, and after all, they were all Gloabons under the skin. *If you tickle us, do we not laugh?* he thought. *If you cut us, do we not ooze?*

The footsteps drew nearer, and Rawlgeeb took a deep breath, resolving to keep his back straight and his chin up. But when the door swung open, there were no armed guards, and only one person stepped forward.

Rawlgeeb knew the insignia of a commander when he saw it, and although he was a civilian employee, he attempted a salute. His visitor eyed him disdainfully, a sneer on her lips, and as silence filled the cell, Rawlgeeb's newfound courage faltered. "Er, hello, ma'am. I'm...I'm Rawlgeeb."

"I know who you are, and I know exactly what you've done," the commander snapped. "My name is Commander Tsumper, and I am here on behalf of the High Command."

"Oh."

Tsumper drew a breath as if marshaling her patience. "Rawlgeeb, you have brought the Gloabon Government into disrepute while on Earth territory, and you have been sentenced to thirty days in the brig pending an inquiry."

Rawlgeeb nodded sadly. "Yes, but there were extenuating circumstances. You see, I didn't know that–"

"Enough! To the prepared mind, there are no unforeseen eventualities."

"Quite so. Sorry."

Tsumper took a step closer to him. "However, there may be a way out of the predicament in which you find yourself. And to earn that opportunity, all you would have to do is serve the Government in a certain capacity. Does that interest you?"

"Definitely," Rawlgeeb replied without hesitation. "I'm always happy to serve the Government. It goes without saying."

"Very good. But sometimes, in order to serve, we must separate from that which we love the most."

An image of Breamell flashed through Rawlgeeb's mind, but the commander couldn't be referring to her, could he? It was hard to know. The Gloabon Intelligence Service was extremely powerful, and its tentacles were far-reaching. Any member of the administration could be monitored at any time, and it was all too possible that they knew about his assignation with Breamell right down to the shoes he'd been wearing when he'd called at her cabin. In a moment of clarity, it occurred to Rawlgeeb that a careless word at this point could land him in very hot water indeed. Events were always open to alternative interpretations, and the less he said the better. He clamped his lips shut and stared straight ahead, dipping his chin to acknowledge the commander's words.

"Would it surprise you," Tsumper went on, "if I told you that human beings were going missing?"

"Missing? From their homes?" Rawlgeeb shook his head. "No, I believe it's quite common."

Tsumper looked him up and down. "Are you making sport with me, Rawlgeeb? Because if you are, I can make sure that your case isn't heard for a long time. A *very* long time. And until then, you'll remain here, or perhaps, you'll be moved to one of the shared cells. I'm sure that there are a few prisoners down here who would be delighted to meet you."

"I intended no offense," Rawlgeeb said hurriedly. "I must have misunderstood. Forgive me. From where are the humans being lost?"

"That's a more intelligent response," Tsumper said. "Perhaps there's hope for you yet." She paused. "The humans are going missing from this very station. Samples that have been brought in and logged by the Earth Liaison Unit are vanishing in large numbers." Tsumper hesitated. "It goes without saying that this fact must remain a secret. To divulge it would be an act of treason punishable by death."

Rawlgeeb swallowed hard. "I understand. But, Commander, with the greatest of respect, we have strict protocols in place to track the humans we bring aboard. Every step of the procedure is logged and time-stamped."

"And yet, two humans who should have been immune were abducted by you ten days ago. One, it turned out was a high-level member of the AGI, the other was an employee of the United Nations."

"Ah, I was given the wrong instructions. There was an administrative error, but I rectified the situation immediately as soon as it came to light. Both humans were safely returned on the same day."

Tsumper shook her head. "Those humans have only just appeared back on Earth."

"What? That can't be right."

Tsumper held up a tablet computer. "I have the records right here. There can be no dispute."

Rawlgeeb felt the color drain from his face. He could almost feel the symbionts withering in his skin. He'd been a cog in the mighty machine that was the Gloabon administration for his entire adult life, and he could recognize this situation for exactly what it was: he was being stitched up. Someone had used him as a pawn in their machinations, and they'd gone to great lengths to do it. *Well played*, he thought. *Whoever you are, you've backed me into a corner and left me nowhere to turn.* A sense of calm came over him, and a sad smile pulled his lips tight. He was screwed, and there was absolutely no point in complaining about it. Whoever had done this, they would've been sure to cover their tracks. Any arguments or protestations at this point would only make him look guilty. He had no choice but to accept his fate.

"I see that you understand," Tsumper went on, "but I do

have a way in which you might redeem yourself."

"Really? Is that even possible?" The words took an age to emerge from Rawlgeeb's mouth. "I don't see how it can be done."

Tsumper's smile was smug. "There are forces at work of which you know nothing. I have the authority to erase the sordid little incident you were involved in down on the planet. I can delete the record of your arrest and wipe the slate clean. A moment ago, you said that you were ready to help, and I take it that you stand by your promise."

"Yes," Rawlgeeb said slowly, though he wasn't sure whether Tsumper had been asking a question or merely making a statement. If Rawlgeeb was being honest with himself, he had to admit that there wasn't much he was sure of. Not very much at all.

"Excellent." Tsumper stood to attention. "Rawlgeeb, I find you guilty of gross incompetence, and I hereby exile you from the Gloabon race. You are herewith stripped of all citizenship, possessions, rights, and responsibilities. You will be dispatched to the nearest planet, in this case, Earth, and you shall make no further contact with the Gloabon Government. Sentence to be carried out immediately."

Rawlgeeb tried to stand still, but his body wouldn't let him. At some level, he understood every word Tsumper had spoken, but he couldn't for the life of him understand how they could possibly apply to him. Yes, he'd expected to be punished, but this? It could not be right. It was unjust, unfair. It was un-Gloabon! *Speak up!* he told himself. *Before it's too late!* But his lips would only move soundlessly, and his legs were suddenly weak and unsteady. He took a deep breath, his hands flapping the air as if trying to swat Tsumper's words away, and finally, he managed to speak: "No, no, no. There must be some mistake. I said I'd help.

You told me that I could redeem myself. You said you'd give me a chance."

Tsumper stepped very close, her voice a hiss. "This *is* your chance to serve, Rawlgeeb. It has to be this way. I need someone outside the system, someone I can rely on to investigate and file regular reports. But I can't trust a human. You must see that."

"I don't understand. This is a ruse?" Rawlgeeb's hands went to his head, his fingers pressing tight against his temples. "Does this mean I'm not really being exiled?"

"Oh, you're being exiled, all right. Thrown out. Disposed of. Sent to purgatory." Tsumper licked her lips as if savoring her extended vocabulary. "But if you play your cards right and help me to find out what's happened to all those missing humans, you'll be reinstated and brought back with full honors."

"Right. I think I understand. I'm being sent undercover." Rawlgeeb clasped his hands together over his stomach, his fingers twined together as if trying to tie themselves in knots. "But...do I really need to be exiled? I mean, couldn't you just *pretend* to banish me?"

"Yes, but this way, if you screw up, I get to deny all knowledge of the whole affair." Tsumper brushed her hands together as if wiping them clean. "There's a human expression for it, but I can't quite put my finger on it. Anyway, the point is, I'll be in the clear. We'll all agree that you were rotten to the core, and I'll be congratulated for banishing you. Win-win, for me at any rate." She brightened. "Right. The resettlement crew is waiting outside. I'd ask them to go easy on you, but that would give the game away. Sorry about that." She headed for the door.

"Wait," Rawlgeeb called out. "They're here already? But

you didn't know that I'd agree to help."

Tsumper half turned. "It didn't really matter. I was going to banish you either way. That's the beauty of it." She strode through the exit, and as she left, three armed guards lumbered inside, a dark hunger in their eyes.

"Right lads," one of them began, "let's get this treacherous little scumbag dealt with."

The other guards chortled quietly, menace crackling in their guttural laughter, and Rawlgeeb closed his eyes and focused on a simple mantra that was as old as the history of sentient life in the galaxy. *Shit!* he thought. *Shit, shit, shit!*

CHAPTER 11

Aboard *The Kreltonian Skull* - Andromeda Class Battle Cruiser

Official Status: Missing and/or Unreachable.

Ship's Log: Earth Orbit.

Chief Engineer Dex exchanged a worried look with Lieutenant Turm. "It's no use, Turm. It's just not working." Dex leaned over the prone figure on the workbench, studying the tracery of wires that connected the newly assembled cybonic lifeform to the bulky, whirring machine on a trolley nearby. "Can you do me a favor? Reach over and increase the current on the metabolic modulator."

Turm stepped up to the machine and pointed to a dial. "This one?"

"No! The blue one. There. Left a bit. Up. No, not that far." He let out a grunt. "Hell's teeth, I'd do it myself, but I need to keep an eye on the auxiliary connections. I've got him wired up like a–"

"Don't say it," Turm interrupted. "I don't mind coming down here to help you out with this, but if you mention Klumzel trees one more time, I swear I'm going to flip."

Dex arched his eyebrows. "I was going to say like a Xircon 73D. What's all this about Klumzel? Are you over-tired or something? You seem on edge."

"I'm sorry, I didn't mean to jump down your throat." Turm ran a hand across her furrowed brow. "Norph has all the senior officers working crazy shift patterns. I don't know what the hell's got into him." She winced as though mildly embarrassed by what she was about to say. "Actually, I have to confess…I've got a selfish reason for wanting our cybonic friend back on his feet. He won't need much downtime, and he can take a few extra shifts. Having him back on active duty would make life one hell of a lot easier for the rest of us."

"All right, let's try again," Dex said gently. "You've got the right dial–the blue one–so just turn it up very gradually, and keep going until I say stop."

"Will do." Turm rotated the dial, her thick fingers moving slowly, a gentle hum rising from the machine as the digits on one of its displays flickered and changed.

Dex leaned even closer to the cybonic lifeform, staring deep into its expressionless eyes. A film of sweat formed on the engineer's upper lip, and he ground his teeth together, every muscle in his jaw tight. This was delicate work and it had to be done right. He had to concentrate, to watch for the moment when the restored neural net synchronized with its new cybonic host. The first sign would be a reaction in the cybonic irises; a narrowing of the pupils as they sensed light for the first time. It was a moment for absolute precision, every setting critical. But he had to admit that there was just one small problem with his method: it wasn't working. Not even a little.

"Flek it!" Dex muttered. "Turn the damned thing all the way to max."

"Are you sure?"

Dex flexed his fingers in the air. "Absolutely! After all, the poor bastard's dead. What have we got to lose?"

"All right, you're the engineer." Turm looked doubtful, but she did as she was told, the drone of the machine rising to a howling, demonic wail. "There. That's as high as it will go. I hope you know what you're doing, Dex."

"Oh yes. No problem." Dex looked back into the lifeform's eyes, barely flinching as a blue spark arced across the erstwhile science officer's skull. "Live!" Dex cackled. "Live, damn you! Live!"

Turm raised her voice over the deafening hum. "It's not having any effect. We should shut it down. You must've made a mistake."

"No. I saw his irises twitch. This is it. You wanted a miracle, and I've given you one. But this is no minor miracle, it's major, Turm. Can you hear me?"

On the workbench, the cybonic lifeform began to shake, its spine arching, its arms and legs rattling against the metallic surface. "Turn it off!" Dex yelled. "We've gone too far. It's too much for his net. We're going to blow his mind!"

But Turm simply stared at him, her eyes round with panic. "I think the panel's overloading. It won't respond. There's nothing I can do."

"Let me at it." In two long strides, Dex was at Turm's side, his sharp eyes darting across the displays. He studied each dial in turn, then in one motion, he raised his fist and smashed it against the side of the machine, the impact booming out across the room. The machine emitted a high-pitched shriek then fell silent, purple smoke pouring from its seams.

"Now *that* looks like a Klumzel tree," Turm said. "Especially with those flames coming out the back."

Dex sighed. "I love the smell of scorched silicon in the morning. It smells to me like circuitry—freshly soldered and ready to test. Ah, it takes me back to my childhood. Happy days."

"In my opinion, that fire should be extinguished immediately," someone said.

Dex grabbed hold of Turm's arm. "Was that you?"

"No," the lieutenant murmured. "It was *him*."

On the workbench, the cybonic lifeform sat up, its movements unnervingly swift. "I don't know what I just had to drink, but somebody get me another. It's party time!"

"Zak3? Is that you?" Dex asked.

"Yes," the lifeform said. "And also, no." The lifeform stood stiffly, plucking the wires from its frame and tossing them aside. "I can detect some legacy protocols left behind by a unit designated Zak3, but all my subroutines have been reconfigured during the reboot. My core systems have carried out an automatic recovery process, repairing and optimizing all of my settings, and I am pleased to report that my neural net is completely operational, and all my circuits are fun...funk...funk...funky, erm..." The lifeform's cheek twitched for a moment. "I am pleased to report that I am perfectly all right." It studied them, its eyes darting from side to side. "Who are you? And what is your purpose?"

Dex frowned. "This our navigation officer, Lieutenant Turm, and I am Chief Engineer Dex."

The lifeform threw back its head. "Ha! Where's Harry? Get it? Where's Harry?"

"Er, there's a Petty Officer Harro in the security team," Dex offered. "Do you want to see him?"

"Oh, for flek's sake, it's a joke," the lifeform said. "Oh well, I guess it's close enough. Turm, Dex, and Harro. Ha!"

"Did he just say flek?" Turm asked. "Zak3 never used to swear like that."

"Some models have an optional profanity circuit," Dex said. "It might have got activated in the repair."

"Query," the lifeform began, "why are you both so ugly? Have you been involved in an accident in the workplace?"

"Oh hell, this is no good," Turm moaned. "He's only going to last for two minutes before Norph blows his head off and throws him out of an airlock."

Dex held up his hands. "Don't worry, it's just a few teething problems. He's probably got a few circuits on the fritz after the reboot. Leave him with me. I'll fix him up."

"Subsequent query–we have established that I am not Zak3, so who am I? What is my nay…nay…" It closed its mouth abruptly, then tried again. "What the actual flek is my flecking name?" Its lips curled in a curious grin. "Interesting. The words *flek* and *flecking* seem to help with my speech capabilities. I must use them more often."

"No!" Turm cried out. "Not on the bridge anyway." She held out her hands to Dex, imploring. "Do something. *Please*."

"Well, perhaps if we give it a name, it'll help it to stabilize," Dex suggested. "You know, it might help him to rebuild his personality."

Turm chewed her lower lip. "Will that work?"

"I can't say for sure," Dex replied. "I'm an engineer, not a psychiatrist, but it's got to be worth a shot." He gave the lifeform a smile. "How about Zak4? Keep it simple."

"No flecking way." The lifeform folded its arms. "I want a new name. One of my own. Also, why do you get to pick out my name? It's so unfair. I'm my own person. And you, you're just a loser. I hate you."

"Hey, I get it," Turm breathed. "He's growing up. A few minutes ago, he was like an infant, asking dumb questions and experimenting with new words. Now, he's going through adolescence."

Dex clapped a hand over his mouth. "You're right. This is incredible. We should be recording all of this. It's never been done before."

"Zeb," the lifeform announced. "From now on, everybody has to call me Zeb."

"All right," Turm said gently. "Zeb it is. I think you ought to rest for a while, Zeb. Take it easy while things settle down."

"What the flek would you know about it?" Zeb demanded. He turned to Dex. "Where's my room? I want to go to my room."

"Fine. I'll show you to your quarters and get you settled in." Dex waved Turm away. "You head back to the bridge. I'll take it from here."

Turm nodded. "Okay, but call me if you need anything."

"I want to be on my ow…ow…ow… Flek it! I want to be by my flecking self!" Zeb intoned, his voice heavy and dull. "You losers are such a pain in the ass."

"Give me strength," Dex murmured. "He'd better get through his teenage years fast, because otherwise, I may have to throw him out of an airlock myself."

CHAPTER 12

Earth

"It's almost five," Brent said as he marched across his office and peered out through the window. "I figured she'd have shown up by now."

Vince looked up from the mound of paperwork that had been keeping him quiet all afternoon. "Maybe she goes straight home after work. She's probably got a husband and three kids waiting for her. A woman like that, she could have any man she wanted. She's probably married to a top politician or some guy who made it big exploiting Gloabon tech. Oh sure, he'll let her keep her little job at the UN, just to give her a hobby, but she won't need the money."

"You're forgetting one thing, Vince. She walked into that crummy diner as a customer, the same as us. What was she doing? Slumming it?"

"And *you're* forgetting that she took one look at you and ran like hell," Vince countered. "And she was quick to call the cops. That's a rich girl tactic if ever I saw one."

Brent shook his head. "I still say you're wrong. When I met her before, there was something she said…"

"Hey, is your memory coming back?"

Brent waggled his hand in the air. "Not really. Just snippets here and there. There are still a lot of gaps. And there's a whole heap of stuff that I ought to remember, but none of it makes any sense to me. Like this sucker, for example." He strolled over to the battered, gray filing cabinet and examined the container of water that sat atop it, peering down at the single, black fish circling within. The creature was oddly fascinating: it's long, trailing fins had a certain elegance as they curled in the water, but any charm that the fish might possess was more than outweighed by the huge eyes that swiveled and bulged on each side of its head. It was as if the fish's body contained a terrible pressure that had forced its eyes from their sockets. "I mean look at it. Are you sure it isn't yours?"

"Positive. Someone gave it to you. A client."

"Man, I must've really pissed them off. I'd have preferred a plant. You know, one of those big ones with all the holes in the leaves." He paused. "Or money. Yes, I'd definitely have preferred a handful of cold, hard cash to this misshapen lump of slimy, wet fish."

"I call it Algernon," Vince put in. "Algy for short. Like algae, get it?"

Brent stared at him.

"Forget it," Vince said defensively. "It's just a joke."

"Almost," Brent admitted, "but not quite." Despite his best intentions, his gaze went back to the fish, unaccountably drawn to its fluid motion as it glided through the murky water. He couldn't keep his eyes off the damned thing. The creature appeared to return the sentiment, gawping back at Brent with something like an accusation in its torpid stare.

"At least I feed the damned thing when you're not around," Vince grumbled. "And by the way, you should get it a proper bowl, or better yet, an aquarium. It's freaky keeping it in that thing."

Brent studied the fish's home: an upturned deep sea diving helmet, its toughened glass visor providing a side view of Algernon's small world to anyone who might want to experience such a visual treat. "I don't know, I think it adds a certain style to the office. Come to think of it though, where the hell did I get a helmet like this? I'm not even sure if I can swim."

"I wish you'd see a doctor or something. You need some help to get your memory back. Apart from anything else, you're driving me crazy." He adopted a drawling tone in a passable imitation of his boss. "Where's this? Where's that? Do I have a car? Where's my clean laundry? Do I smoke? Am I married? Do I prefer cats or dogs?" He heaved a sigh. "There's no end to it. You *need* to see a doctor."

"Doctors! What do they know?" Brent let out a humorless laugh. "Besides, I don't even know if I have medical insurance yet, and getting back a lifetime of memories…that could work out expensive. Anyway, why should I bother when it's all coming back by itself?"

Vince snorted. "Yeah, it's *so* much more *fun* this way." He tutted under his breath. "And before you ask again, the helmet was another gift from an old client. And when I say a *gift*, I mean *a warning*. I got quite a surprise when that damned thing came in through the window."

"Don't tell me–the window was closed at the time."

"Yeah," Vince went on, "and the helmet was kind of heavy, especially as there was still someone's head inside it."

Brent rubbed his jaw, thinking. He seemed to have a pretty strange clientele. It was a wonder he'd stayed in business this long. But then he caught the smirk sidling onto Vince's expression and realization dawned. "Okay, *that* was a joke. You caught me fair and square."

Vince looked as though he was about to contradict him, but Brent didn't give him the chance. He didn't want to live in a world where a severed head arriving through the window would only be mentioned as an afterthought if it came up in conversation. Right now, there was only so much reality he could take. "Maybe you should go home, Vince.

Take the rest of the day off."

"I was *supposed* to finish work half an hour ago," Brent said, then he cocked his ear. "Wait, someone's coming up the stairs. Sounds like someone in heels. Could be her."

Brent straightened his jacket and affected a nonchalant pose, leaning against the filing cabinet, his arms folded. Algernon goggled at him, its eyeballs swiveling in a disdainful fashion. "Shut up," Brent muttered. "Everyone's a goddamned critic."

His one-sided conversation was interrupted by a polite knock on the door, and Brent unfolded his arms and hurriedly smoothed down his unruly hair. "Get the door on your way out, Vince."

"Aw, but I wanted to stay. This feels like we could be onto something. Something big."

Brent shook his head. "What you need to remember, Vince, is Bolster's first law."

"And what's that?"

"All conspiracy theories are the work of one man," Brent said with a smile. "Now, you can stay if you want to, but it's on your own time. I'm running a business here, not an entertainment for young men of no noticeable talent. And you still have to get the door, all right?"

"Fine." Vince scowled and trudged from his desk, but when he opened the door, his frown miraculously blossomed into a wide smile, his eyes gleaming with gladness. "Ms. Richmond! What an absolute pleasure to see you again. Please, do come in."

Maisie stepped into the room, and the dreary office suddenly seemed to come alive with a golden glow. Gone was the damp-stained ceiling; its bulging plaster lost in the playful warmth of dappled light. The sagging wallpaper vanished; its faded pattern replaced by a subtle patchwork of pastel hues. And to Brent, the threadbare carpet of indeterminate color became the floor of the finest ballroom; its dark wooden boards gleaming with the delicate sheen of polished opulence. And as his heart soared, Brent stiffened his spine, and standing tall, he extended his arm in a welcoming gesture and said, "How, how, how nice…to see that you are…that you are here." He forced a smile, thinking, *Goodbye, self-esteem. It was nice knowing you.*

But if Maisie could tell that he was cringing inside, she was gracious enough not to let it show. Instead, she favored him with a generous smile. "Mr. Bolster, we need to talk. Is now a good time?"

"Now is a very good time," Brent replied, making a valiant effort to keep his tongue from flopping out of his mouth in the manner of an overheated Labrador. "Vince, fetch Ms. Richmond a…thing with legs. To sit on." He caught Vince's frown and added, "Please."

"Certainly, Mr. Bolster," Vince said with just the slightest roll of his eyes. "My pleasure." He fetched the only spare chair, positioning it in the center of the room, and when he brushed down the seat with the palm of his hand, it kicked up a small cloud of dust.

Maisie went to sit down but hesitated. "Oh, is that…is that a blood stain?"

"Certainly not," Vince replied. "It's only an imperfection in the leather. I cleaned the blood off just last week."

"Right," Maisie said slowly, but she sat down, tucking her skirt around her thighs as she did so, and arranging her long legs demurely beneath the chair.

Brent's racing pulse had been booming in his ears, but

now it was suddenly absent, and he laid his hand on his chest as if searching for signs of life. *Get a grip!* he scolded himself, but it was no use. Out in the street or at a distance across a crowded restaurant, he'd known that Maisie Richmond could turn heads, stop traffic, and charm the birds from the sky. But at close quarters and in the confines of his cramped office, she cast a spell on him with such force that his very existence seemed knocked out of kilter, his senses reeling. Brent struggled to regain his composure, and as his heart resumed its regular rhythm, a host of mental images came back to him: Maisie emerging from deep shadows; Maisie in a deep blue dress; Maisie in a dark room. A room with bars at the door. "Holy shit!" he breathed. "We were abducted!"

Meeting his startled gaze with an expression of cool certainty, Maisie nodded. "Yes. It took me a while to figure it out too. I knew something was wrong, but I didn't know what to do about it. In fact, if I hadn't bumped into you earlier at the diner, I don't know if I'd have managed to work it out at all."

"So, in the diner, why did you run?" Brent asked. "I know you recognized me, so why did you take off?"

She bowed her head slightly. "I'm sorry. You're right, I did recognize you, but I only knew that you belonged to a memory I'd buried. I didn't know *how* I knew you. I was sure that I'd been missing for several days, but as far as I was concerned, you might've been the one who'd kidnapped me or held me somewhere against my will."

"But you didn't say that to the cops," Brent argued.

"What can I say?" Maisie raised her hands then let them fall in her lap. "When I saw you standing there, I somehow knew that you weren't a threat. I guess you seemed familiar, and I started to recollect our previous encounter, but the full memory didn't come back to me until this afternoon."

"I get what you're saying," Vince put in. "Brent hasn't been able to remember much since he went missing. An awful lot of his marbles went walkabout in those ten days."

Maisie gasped. "You were gone for ten days too? That's the same for me. Ten whole days just wiped out as though they never happened." She hesitated, tears moistening her eyes. "I'll admit it...I'm afraid. I'm afraid of what might've happened to me in that time. I've got to find out. However bad it is, I have to know. Do you think you could help me? I mean, you are an investigator, and I'm sure you must be a good one. You certainly managed to track me down to that diner." A delicate chuckle slipped from her ruby lips. "It's a trashy place, I know, but I kind of like it. I've no idea how you managed to find me so quickly."

"Actually–" Vince began, but Brent talked over him, raising his voice.

"Thank you, Vince, but I'm sure Ms. Richmond understands that as a qualified investigator and a platinum level member of the AGI, I couldn't possibly divulge the secrets of my trade."

"I suppose not," Maisie said. "And please, call me Maisie. After all, we're going to be working together."

Brent wrinkled his nose. "Not so much *together*. I work alone unless you count Vince here, which, speaking personally, I try not to do. But don't get me wrong–I'm happy to take you on as a client. I'll have to check, but I think my usual daily rates are–"

"Waived in this particular case," Vince interrupted, meeting Brent's glare with one of his own. "Never let it be said that Bolster and Associate Investigations took advantage of someone who needed our help."

"Wait a minute!" Brent's faculties were recovering quickly now, and he distinctly remembered a few important terms that he'd normally bandy about at this point in the proceedings. Not just the daily rates and extra charges for night work, but magical phrases like travel allowances, subsistence payments, and sundry expenditures. As the words crept into his mind, he greeted them like old friends, and in turn, they introduced him to their fellows: uncategorized expenses, miscellaneous outgoings, and early completion bonuses. All of these things, he felt instinctively, were very close to his heart, and he should not be expected to abandon them in favor of the prudish little expression: *pro bono*.

Vince strode closer to Brent, his solid frame blocking Maisie from view, and Brent couldn't help but notice the way Vince's shoulders strained the seams of his jacket almost to bursting point. "Listen for a second," Vince began. "You wanted to crack this mystery before we even knew about Ms. Richmond. You *need* to solve it. It's in your interest to find out what happened, so you need this case just as much as she does."

"All right, goddammit!" Brent shoved past Vince and plastered his best smile across his face. "Ms. Richm– that is, Maisie. I will be delighted to take your case. It would be my honor to help you in any way I can." He shot a look at Vince. "Perhaps you could fetch Maisie a drink."

"Sure," Vince said. "I think there's some coffee left."

"Ooh, do you have tea?" Maisie asked. "English Breakfast if you have it. That's my favorite."

"Mine too," Brent crooned. "Vince, why don't you run along to the store and fetch some of that delicious tea for our guest?"

"All right, why not?" Vince held out his hand but when

all he received was a blank look from Brent, he added, "Cash? For the tea?"

Brent waved him aside. "I'm sure you can take care of it, now that you're my *associate*."

Vince's shoulders slumped, and he headed for the door. "Don't get too far ahead without me," he said over his shoulder. "And take notes. Lots of notes." He shut the door with more force than was called for, and his heavy tread could be heard in the office as he stomped down the stairs.

"To business." Brent settled himself at his desk, brushing the careful piles of paperwork aside with a sweep of his arm. "Where were you when you were abducted?"

"I *think* I was just coming away from a fundraiser," Maisy offered. "The next thing I knew, I was waking up back at home all dressed up to the nines. I was confused, but I knew I was supposed to be at work, so I showered and changed and headed across town. I was starving, so I stopped off at the diner, and that's pretty much all I know. How about you?"

"The same. Only without the fundraiser, the regular job, the fancy clothes, and…" Brent gave the air an experimental sniff. "I'm pretty sure I didn't stop to shower either."

"So, completely different then."

Brent shrugged. "We were both supposed to be immune, but we were both taken. We have that in common. That and the ten missing days. We just need a lead, something to go on." He drummed his fingers on the desk, feeling sharper by the minute. It felt good to be working a case. He could do this; it was his territory. "So, you went back to work. Anything weird there? Anything out of place? Someone with a grudge maybe?"

"No. Nothing like that."

"Excuse me being personal, but I have to rule out the usual suspects," Brent said. "For instance, do you have a jealous husband at home? Or maybe an over-emotional fiancée? A boyfriend?"

Maisie's smile was coy, but there was a glint in her eye. "I know you're fishing, Mr. Bolster, so I shouldn't even answer, but for the record, I'm single. My work takes up all my time."

"And what work is that, exactly?"

"I'm a researcher, studying the impact on Earth of the Gloabon arrival." Maisie leaned forward, warming to her subject. "I'm especially interested in the economic and political issues that have arisen since the Gloabons arrived, and I'm undertaking a long-term study of the way the Gloabons have influenced patterns of human activity. You know, working lives, settlement, migration. All the usual stuff."

Brent pursed his lips. "I understand exactly what you're talking about, but we'll need a simpler version for Vince. He's a little slow on the uptake if you know what I mean. He was involved with a college football team, and he took a few bumps on the head."

"Ah, he certainly has the right build for it. What was he, a fullback?"

Brent blinked. "Oh, he didn't play. I think they used him for a tackling sled. You know, those guys could charge into Vince all day long and never knock him down—not once. But let's get back to it. The one-line version of your job description might be something like, you try to figure out how come our Gloabon overlords are still calling all the shots, even though we've got them outnumbered. Am I right?"

Maisie sighed. "You ever heard of the Aztecs?"

"Of course, the Aztec family own that chain of Mexican

restaurants." Brent patted his stomach. "That reminds me, I never did get to finish my chili."

"You're just being obtuse. The Aztecs ruled their part of the world because they had the best weapons available — clubs with shards of volcanic glass set into the sides. But along came the Spaniards with steel and gunpowder, and the Aztecs were doomed." She folded her arms. "You must know that Gloabon tech is way ahead of anything we ever had on Earth. If they'd wanted to invade, we'd have been wiped out in no time at all."

Brent grimaced. "I'd have liked to see them try."

"No, you wouldn't. Look what happened to the UK."

"That was a shame," Brent admitted. "I always wanted to visit London." His expression brightened. "Still, on the plus side, I hear all their politicians got zapped, so most folks are probably better off."

Maisie pressed the fingers of one hand against her temple. "I'll tell you what, Brent. Let's just say that I study the way things have turned out since the Gloabons arrived and leave it at that."

"Sure, why not?" Brent took a breath. "So, here's what happened to me. I was home in my apartment, fast asleep, when the Gloabon showed up. It's coming back to me now. He was a funny guy or thought he was. Liked to run off at the mouth. Green. He had a real weird name too. Something like a widget you use when you're putting a shelf up."

Maisie's hand flew to her mouth. "I know what you mean. I had the same guy. And he came to the cell later to let you out. What was he called? Bracket? Drill bit? Ratchet?"

"Almost!" Brent's fingers combed the air as if he could pull the right word from the ether, drawing it out from an invisible chaos. "It definitely started with an R. Router? Rebate?" He sat suddenly still, his eyes locked on Maisie's. "I have it. It was Rawlplug!"

Maisie's face lit up with a jubilant smile. And all hell broke loose.

Something slammed into the office door with a mighty crash, and a raucous roar of anger split the air, followed a split second later by a harsh yelp of pain.

Brent jumped to his feet. "Maisie, get behind me."

Maisie leaped from her chair, and Brent yanked open his desk drawer, searching for a weapon that his instincts told him must be there. But before he could find it, the door burst open and a tall figure strode into the room.

The Gloabon was tall and thin, his eyes burning with fury. And he was stark naked. He lifted his long, thin arm and pointed at Brent. "My name," he yelled, his voice filled with venom, "is *Rawlgeeb! RAWLGEEB!* And I will have my vengeance upon you, human!"

Brent clicked his fingers. "Rawlgeeb! Yes, that's it."

"Seriously?" Maisie hissed. "That's what you're getting from this?"

Rawlgeeb staggered closer, his arm still outstretched. "They took everything from me. Everything! They took my badge, my tablet, my handset. All of it. Then they stripped me. They beat me. And they...they...did things. Things no Gloabon should ever do to another." He let out a wail of anguish mixed with unbridled rage. "And they *laughed* at me."

"I'm sorry to hear that," Brent said, keeping his voice level. "That sounds real bad. Especially the, er, the..." He cleared his throat and leaned forward, letting his hands creep farther into the drawer. *Where the hell is that damned gun?* But there was nothing there except for crumpled balls

99

of paper and small fragments of something crumbly that lodged beneath his nails as he scrabbled through the detritus. *I hope those are just cookie crumbs or something like that*, he thought. But aloud, he said, "Tell me about this badge. I didn't know you guys had badges. What was it, gold or what?"

"What does it matter what it was made of? It was my badge of rank. It was everything I've worked for, everything I *was*."

Brent managed a strained smile. "You're being too hard on yourself. You know, work isn't everything."

"It is to all good Gloabons," Rawlgeeb spluttered. "But...I'm not a Gloabon anymore. They took that too. I'm just a...a nothing."

Brent's fingers found an edge of cold metal, and he recognized the feel of the alien weapon he'd been given many years ago. Grasping the gun firmly, he whipped it up, pointing it at Rawlgeeb's chest. "Haha! Back off, my green and very angry little friend. Don't make me use this."

"Go ahead," Rawlgeeb sneered. "For one thing, it's not loaded. You can tell by the blue light on the side."

Brent narrowed his eyes. "You're bluffing. You can't kid a kidder."

"For another thing," Rawlgeeb went on, "I don't have any papers I need fastening together at the moment. And that's what that particular device is for, in case you hadn't grasped my meaning. I'm spelling it out for you because you seem to be some kind of moron."

In the silence that followed, nothing moved except for the beads of sweat trickling down Brent's brow. "This gun was a gift from an old client. I don't think he'd have fobbed me off with some piece of useless junk." He set his mouth in a grim line, his expression hard, but from the corner of his eye, he caught sight of Algernon in his ridiculous bowl, and his confidence evaporated. He couldn't remember much about his old clients, but something told him they were a bunch of slippery bastards, not to be trusted under any circumstances.

"I have spent a lifetime in administration," Rawlgeeb snarled, "and if there's one thing we don't joke about, its office equipment." Rawlgeeb craned his long neck toward Brent, and now his voice was a rasping whisper: "The GM-903 is the most powerful stapler in your world. It takes heavy-duty ten-millimeter staples that can go clean through a hundred sheets of A4. But I know what you're thinking. Maybe you fired the whole clip, or maybe there's still one shot left in the mechanism. So what you've got to ask yourself is, do I feel lucky? Well do you, Brent? Do you feel lucky?"

"Shit!" Brent tossed the staple gun onto his desk. "I guess we'll have to do this the hard way." He pulled back his sleeves and adopted a fighting stance. "You asked for this, pal."

Rawlgeeb tilted his head to one side, the vertebrae crackling in his neck. "As you wish, but I hope you've remembered that even as an exiled Gloabon, I can still punch with twenty-five times more force than the average human."

"Yeah, I knew that, obviously," Brent said. "But I know something that you don't."

"I doubt that very much indeed." Rawlgeeb raised his own fists and bared his teeth.

"Believe it. Because my friend Vince is a damned sight tougher than the average human, and while you were ranting about staple guns, he was walking in the door. He's standing behind you right now."

Rawlgeeb froze, but before he could turn around, Vince crashed into him, sending him sprawling to the floor and landing on top of him. Vince's clothes were ripped, there was a graze on one side of his head, and his face was puce with anger. He pinned Rawlgeeb to the ground and sat astride him, holding his opponent's arms in a vice-like grip. "Jump me when I'm not looking, would you?" Vince roared. "Sneak up behind me, would you? I'll teach you a lesson, you bastard!"

"Woah!" Brent called out. "Take it easy, Vince. We want him alive."

"I was bringing the tea!" Vince hollered. "*Tea* goddammit! You don't jump a guy when he's running up the stairs with nothing on him but a goddamned packet of Earl Grey!"

"Oh, was there no English Breakfast?" Maisie murmured, but when Vince turned his gaze on her, she smiled and said, "Thank you anyway, Vince. Earl Grey is fine. Lovely."

Rawlgeeb struggled for a second, then he seemed to deflate. "All right, you win. I was suffering from the Gom Hafir for a while, but it's passed."

"What's that?" Vince asked leaning back as far as he could while still holding Rawlgeeb down. "You don't have some kind of weird alien disease, do you? Because I have allergies."

"It's a kind of blood rage," Maisie put in. "The Gom Hafir is a phenomenon usually associated with Gloabon warriors. It's kind of like a red mist, and it only occurs in extreme circumstances." She paused. "We're probably the only humans to have witnessed it. Well, the only ones who've lived to tell the tale, anyway. It's just as well he wasn't armed."

"Please, you can let me go," Rawlgeeb mumbled. "I won't cause you any more trouble. I was supposed to come here to talk, but after what happened I…I must've snapped. Don't worry. I'll leave quietly if you let me go."

"Hold on a second," Brent said. "You wanted to talk to us, and I reckon that goes both ways. If your gummy heifer is all done messing with your mind, we might just be able to salvage something from this train wreck. Play ball with us, and I'll make sure Vince here doesn't rip your arms and legs off."

"I doubt whether he could," Rawlgeeb replied. "My joints are much tougher than yours."

"Doesn't mean he wouldn't have a great deal of fun trying," Brent countered. "Now, what do you say? We'll set you free, and in return, you'll help us out by answering a few questions."

Rawlgeeb took a steadying breath. "All right. What choice do I have? I may as well go along with it. It seems to be my day for helping people out."

Brent strolled around his desk and patted Vince on the shoulder. "You did good, kid, but you can get off him now."

Vince looked doubtful, but he hauled himself off the alien then stood back, his face falling when he noticed the state of his own clothes. "This is my best jacket, and it's ruined."

"Vince, that's your *only* jacket," Brent said, "and it was ruined when some poor sweatshop sap first put a needle and thread to it. I'll tell you what, get yourself a new suit, and I'll take it out of your wages."

"Thanks." Vince started to smile but it didn't last long. "Very funny. How about you pay me a fat bonus for saving your ass from an outraged alien, *and* you give me compensation for my damaged clothes. Otherwise, I might just have a blood rage of my own one of these fine days, and then we'll see what might get hurled through the window."

"Gentlemen," Maisie said firmly, "and gentle, er, being, I think it's time we all calmed down and talked rationally for a while." She stepped closer to Rawlgeeb. "Please get up. Do you need anything?"

Rawlgeeb sat up slowly. "Some clothes would be nice."

They all looked at Vince. Even Algernon.

"You have to be kidding," Vince moaned.

"He's very tall and your clothes are the only ones that might fit," Brent said. "And like you said, they're pretty beat up anyhow."

"Fine. Just goddamned fine!" Vince pulled off his jacket and tossed it to Rawlgeeb.

Brent made an encouraging gesture. "Shirt and pants too."

Vince glared with a ferocity Brent had never seen before. "What?"

"Give the guy some dignity," Brent said. "He needs to cover himself up." Brent shuddered. "Besides, he's giving me the creeps."

"Do you want me to turn around to preserve your modesty?" Maisie asked, lifting her eyebrows just a fraction, a mischievous grin flickering across her lips.

Vince didn't reply. In silence, and with a face like thunder, he removed his pants and shirt, dropping them on the floor, then he trudged over to his desk and sat down, his arms folded. "Happy now?"

Rawlgeeb dressed quickly then stood, Vince's clothes hanging generously from his angular frame. "Thank you.

You're very kind. It's more than I have a right to expect."

"Damned straight," Vince growled.

Brent perched on the edge of his desk. "Maisie, why don't you take your seat, and we'll get back to business."

"Hmm?" Maisie asked absently, her gaze lingering on Vince. "Tell me, do you work out or is that just your natural physique?"

"Don't confuse the lad with long words," Brent said, gesturing firmly to the chair in the center of the room. "Please, sit down. Rawlplug, do you want my chair?"

Rawlgeeb stiffened. "For the last time, it's *Rawlgeeb*, and no, thank you, but I prefer to stand."

"Fine." Brent studied the Gloabon for a second. "You know what? That damned jacket looks better on you than it did on Vince. I think it must be the green skin, it kind of offsets the hideous pattern."

"That jacket is linen and silk," Vince said. "Cost me a fortune."

Rawlgeeb plucked at the jacket's lapel and gave it an experimental sniff. "Synthetic. Polyester and…let me see. Yes, more polyester." He looked at Vince, perhaps recognizing a kindred spirit, and added, "Don't worry. When all this is sorted out, I'll have it cleaned and repaired, and I'll send it back to you."

Vince's frown turned into a guarded smile. "Thanks," he muttered gruffly. "Appreciate it." He turned to Brent. "So how far did you get before we were interrupted? Did you take notes?"

Brent tapped the side of his head. "It's all in here. Maisie was just telling me how she was abducted then wound up at home. Er, what was your address again?"

"I didn't give it," Maisie replied.

"Exactly. That's why I didn't remember it." Brent beamed at Vince. "You see, it's a perfect system."

"Forgive me," Rawlgeeb began, "but we find that humans are often quite confused immediately after sampling. Your memories will return in full over the coming days, but in the meantime, perhaps I could help by filling in the gaps."

Maisie clapped her hands together. "That would be wonderful. For a start, why were we abducted? We should have been immune."

"In your case, you're correct," Rawlgeeb replied. "As a UN employee, you should never have been taken, but I was given incorrect instructions. It *could* have been an error, but I believe it was deliberate. Someone wanted you taken, and when the truth was discovered, they wanted you sent back as if nothing had happened."

"Then why did I lose ten days?" Maisie asked, a tremor creeping into her voice. "Where have I been for the last week and a half?"

"That, I cannot answer," Rawlgeeb replied sadly. "But perhaps we can piece it together."

"What about me?" Brent demanded. "You admitted Maisie shouldn't have been taken, but you said *in your case*. Are you implying I *should* have been abducted?"

Rawlgeeb nodded firmly. "Your AGI license had expired. You were fair game."

"Expired!" Brent spluttered. "I'll have you know that I'm a fully paid-up platinum member."

"That happened afterward. Someone bailed you out, so to speak. That's why I had to go down to the cells and send you home. It was most annoying." Rawlgeeb heaved a sigh. "I was in the bath at the time. Everything was going so well."

A memory swam to the surface of Brent's mind. Yes, his

membership had been bought and paid for by someone un-known. It was all coming back to him. And it could only mean one thing. "Someone's trying to use me. They've paid up front, and one day soon they'll come to collect."

"That still doesn't explain the ten days," Maisie said. "Where were we? What happened to us?"

"I'm not sure that even matters," Brent replied. "The point is, someone wanted me wound up and ready to go. They gave me the tools for the job, then they made sure I had an ax to grind. Hell, they maybe even sent our green friend here to point us in the right direction. For all I know, they put that flyer on my desk and sent me to Martha's go-dawful diner."

"Aren't you forgetting Bolster's first law?" Vince asked.

Brent frowned. "What? You mean, always check there's toilet paper before you commit?"

"No! The one about conspiracy theories being the work of one man," Vince protested. "And also, *ew!*"

A strange barking sound erupted from Rawlgeeb. "The work of one man! I like that. Very good. Very drole."

"Right." Brent rubbed his hands together in a way that he hoped would make him look purposeful and dynamic. "But whoever paid for that upgrade, they also gave me something else. They gave me a lead."

"Can you trace the payment?" Maisie asked.

"Definitely. Vince, work your magic."

"Already on it." Vince had pulled a slim laptop from his desk drawer, and his fingers blurred as he typed. "Wow! You won't believe this."

Brent stood tall, excitement jangling through his nerves. "What? Who paid? Was it a mobster? A crime syndicate? A drug cartel?"

"No!" Vince clapped a hand across his brow. "It was the Mayor."

"The mayor's office?" Brent shook his head. "What am I—a public utility?"

"No, that's just it," Vince said. "It was nothing to do with his office. Mayor Enderley paid your fee from his personal account. It's all right here."

"All right then," Brent drawled. "I guess that gives us a line of inquiry. Hop aboard, people. First stop, the mayor's office."

CHAPTER 13

Gloabon Space Station *The Gamulon* - Earth Orbit

Commander Tsumper glared at the drone footage playing out on her screen. "Rawlgeeb!" she growled. "What the hell do you think you're doing?"

A vein throbbed in her temple as she watched the jumpy images of Rawlgeeb strolling along a street in the company of three humans. The idiot was supposed to be undercover for flek's sake, but here he was, rubbing shoulders with the very people he was supposed to be investigating. *He's cracked up*, she decided. *The banishment was too much for him. He was never the sharpest tool in the box, but now he's become…what?*

She shook her head in disbelief. Rawlgeeb looked utterly ridiculous. He was wearing what appeared to be a bizarre, primitive robe, hugging the loose folds of torn fabric around his thin body as he walked. *Could it be a disguise?* Tsumper frowned. It seemed unlikely, but perhaps Rawlgeeb was under the impression that he could pass himself off as some kind of shaman or mystic. Humans had a particularly skewed view of Gloabon habits and customs, their perceptions muddled by decades of misguided TV shows. It wasn't unknown for Gloabon teenagers to go down to Earth and act out melodramatic scenes, pretending to exercise mind control over each other or sniffing appreciatively at passing humans and pronouncing them almost ripe and ready to harvest. One enterprising gang had cocooned themselves in shrouds of plastic film and pretended to be hibernating, waiting until they'd gathered a good crowd before bursting out and screaming the place down. *Totally inappropriate*, Tsumper thought. *And at Christmas, too*. The humans valued their rituals, and at that time of year they tried hard to create the happy memories they so desperately needed, but that was one Christmas parade that so many would try to forget.

"Rawlgeeb is no teenager though," Tsumper murmured. "He can't have gone that far off the rails so quickly. He must be playing a long game. That has to be it." She took a deep breath and cross-referenced the drone's position with a three-dimensional map to see where the strange party was headed. *Interesting*. The humans were taking Rawlgeeb into an exclusive district. The tree-lined avenues were wide and welcoming, but the tall fences topped with razor wire advertised a different message. This was the exclusive realm of government offices and corporate headquarters, so whoever they were visiting, it had to be someone important or influential. Perhaps Rawlgeeb was on to something after all.

A thin smile lightened Tsumper's expression, but then Rawlgeeb did something she wasn't expecting. He stopped suddenly and turned around, sniffing the air. His eyes narrowed and he seemed to stare straight at her. He'd evidently detected the drone. "He's going to send me a message," Tsumper whispered. Rawlgeeb glanced away for a moment as if in conversation with the larger human, the one in a badly fitting tracksuit, then he looked back at the drone, waiting. Tsumper zoomed the camera in until Rawlgeeb's narrow face filled the screen, and then slowly, deliberately Rawlgeeb raised his middle finger.

"Gagh!" Tsumper's throat tightened, a roar building in her chest. "Insubordination!" she hissed. "I'll make him pay for that! I'll have him banished to the farthest outreaches of the galaxy! I'll–" But her flow of invective stopped short when the image on her screen flickered and died. Rawlgeeb, with the help of the humans, had jammed her signal.

Tsumper closed her eyes. Now that Rawlgeeb knew she was trying to monitor his movements, he would be almost impossible to trace. His years in the Earth Liaison Unit would've taught him everything he needed to know about Gloabon methods of surveillance. If he wanted to, he could become invisible. "He's a ghost," Tsumper whispered. "A renegade. A rogue agent. And I'm the one who sent him down there."

But Tsumper hadn't spent her whole life clawing her way up through the ranks only to be outsmarted by a second-rate administrator, and when she opened her eyes, they glowed bright with a glittering anger. She would regain control of the situation. In her experience, anyone could be manipulated once their pressure points had been discovered, and when it came to Rawlgeeb, she knew exactly where to squeeze.

She tapped the communicator icon on her control pad, and her call was answered immediately, a sleek Gloabon female appearing on her screen. Tsumper smiled. "Surrana, I have a task for you. Is this a good time to talk?"

"I always have time for you," the female purred. "What can I help you with today?"

"I'd like you to pick someone up as soon as possible."

"Shall I ask nicely?" Surrana asked. "Or would you prefer it if I played a little rough?"

"Oh, the latter. Definitely. I want the target unbalanced, so it's a snatch job. Fast and brutal."

"Sounds like fun." Surrana smiled, and despite the sense of distance provided by the screen, a shudder ran down Tsumper's spine. In moments like this, Surrana's intense gaze was utterly frightening and yet strangely alluring. To look into her eyes was to know the true meaning of the word merciless, and for many, Surrana's smile was the last thing they ever saw. "Do you want the target kept alive?" Surrana asked. "Or can I break them?"

Tsumper sucked her teeth. "Alive. At first, anyway. Maybe later, when I've finished, you can have your fun but not yet."

Surrana pouted. "Aw, what a shame. But I shall do as you wish, the same as always. There's just one thing. You haven't told me who the target will be, you silly thing."

"Oh, of course. She's right here on *The Gamulon*. Her name is Breamell."

CHAPTER 14

Aboard *The Kreltonian Skull* - Andromeda Class Battle Cruiser

Official Status: Missing, Unreachable and/or Malfunctioning.

Ship's Log: Earth Orbit.

Chief Engineer Dex unlocked the door to the science officer's quarters, took a long breath, and then let himself in.

Zeb sat quietly at the workstation, his back straight, his attention fixed on the screen. Without looking up, he said, "Greetings, Dad. How's it going?"

"Fine." Dex crossed the cabin and stood behind Zeb's shoulder. "But, you have to stop calling me that."

Zeb tilted his head. "All right. I shall remember that from now on, Chief Engineer Dex."

"Great."

"Unless you'd prefer *Daddy*," Zeb went on. "Or *Pops*, or *The Old Man*."

"No," Dex groaned. "We've been through all this before." He clenched and unclenched his fists. Each time he thought he was getting somewhere with Zeb, the science officer's development went off at a tangent, as if his mind was on a roller coaster, riding a car that was barely attached to the track. "If you're not sure, just stick to using ranks when you speak to someone. If the person is an officer, don't forget to say *sir*. And be respectful."

"Understood. Your rank, for example, is lieutenant commander, correct?"

"Technically, yes, although in the Andelian Fleet, the officer in my role is usually referred to as the chief engineer.

It's a tradition."

Zeb nodded. "According to my memory banks, my rank is also that of lieutenant commander. Logically, it seems that I don't have to obey your orders."

"It doesn't quite work like that," Dex said quickly. "Anyway, that was Zak3's rank, not yours."

"I understand." Zeb looked thoughtful. "I believe that I will revert to my original name and rank with immediate effect. It is time for me to resume my position on the bridge. The ship needs a science officer, and I have been running through the training program at an accelerated rate. I believe that I am now fully qualified."

Dex hesitated. "I'm sorry, but you can't just go back to being Zak3. The admiral…well, there's no easy way to say this—Admiral Norph killed your predecessor, and if he thinks that you are Zak3, he will be very angry."

"He will attempt to kill me?"

"Yes. But the word *attempt* doesn't come into it. He will definitely demolish you, probably in some strange and incredibly painful way. And then he'll figure out that you've been rebuilt, and he'll know that I did the work, and he'll punish me severely. And Lieutenant Turm–she'll be punished too."

Zeb's hand flew to his mouth. "He'd hurt Mom! Oh my God! I cannot allow that to happen."

"She's not–" Dex began, but then changed his mind. "Yes. He'd hurt your mom."

Zeb stood. "I won't let him. I'll stop him."

"The best way to do that," Dex said soothingly, "is to keep quiet about where you came from."

"No. From what you've said, I can only conclude that Admiral Norph is criminally insane. Further, my analysis of the ship's personnel records suggests that he may well be a sociopath. He must be stopped."

Dex waved his hands downward, his fingers spread wide. "Take it easy, Zeb. Yes, Norph probably is a sociopath, but in the Andelian High Command, that's really not all that unusual. Back on Andel, Field Marshal Sumbago is remembered as a hero, his face is on the ten credit notes for flek's sake, but he's known to have eaten at least three of his fellow officers. The title of his autobiography is *Guzzle Your Way to Success*. Can you see where I'm going with this?"

"Yes. I understand that the people of Andel are savages, obsessed with war, violence, and death. I have studied their history. It didn't take very long."

Dex heaved a sigh. "I can see we need to get you socialized. You can't judge an entire species from a few dates in a history file. It's not all wars and battles."

"Two hundred and thirty-seven wars, ninety-eight skirmishes, seventy-two military interventions, fifty-four–"

"Never mind that," Dex interrupted. "The point is that our people have come a long way. We've become a less belligerent species, and we've formed an alliance with the Kreitians to ensure a long-lasting peace. We're entering an age of prosperity. At least, we were until Norph broke us away from the Andel-Kreit fleet. I hate to think what he's cooking up, but it isn't going to be a picnic."

"One moment." Zeb's eyes darted rapidly from side to side. "Checking ship's logs. Analyzing navigational data. Correlating comms traffic with behavioral analysis." He froze, staring at Dex. "I must inform you that in all probability, Admiral Norph is planning to disrupt the Andel-Kreit coalition, plunging the galaxy into unrest. There is little doubt that he hopes to capitalize on the ensuing chaos."

"Sounds about right," Dex admitted, "but there's not a lot we can do about it. Not right now. Norph is no fool, and he knows that the troops on board will do as they're told. All we can do is keep our heads down and see how it plays out."

"A waiting game?" Zeb asked.

Dex nodded. "Yes. There may be something we can do farther down the line, but for now, all anyone needs to know is this: your name is Zeb, you're the new science officer, and you've just been activated. If anyone asks about Zak3, just say that you don't know what happened to him."

"That would be untrue. My neural net will not allow me to lie."

"Yes, it will," Dex stated. "You are programmed to adapt to social norms, and more importantly, you have modules that will always prioritize the preservation of life. And that includes your own life."

"So, I can lie to save my own skin." Zeb raised his left eyebrow. "Neat." He stood to attention. "I'm ready. I need to start learning these social norms you mentioned. I can see how they will enable me to fit in. I must complete my induction process and then take my post on the bridge. Once I'm at my post, it will be a simple matter to study Admiral Norph at close quarters. I must assess his strengths and weaknesses if we are to stop him."

The chief engineer exhaled noisily. "No! Have you not been listening to a single word I've said? If you go against Norph in any way, he'll destroy you. For flek's sake, he killed Zak3 for grinning at him."

"Don't worry." Zeb patted Dex on the shoulder. "You didn't raise a quitter, Dad. One way or another, I'll stop Norph. It's the only thing I can do."

CHAPTER 15

Earth

"You're sure it was a Gloabon drone?" Brent asked. He turned around, peering along the street. A handful of huge cars purred past, their occupants invisible behind heavily tinted glass, but apart from Vince, Maisie, and Rawlgeeb, there was no one else on the sidewalk.

"I'm certain," Rawlgeeb stated. "The fuel cells give off a distinct aroma. I'd know them anywhere."

"That's some sense of smell you have there," Vince said. "Plenty of people would be very keen to take advantage of it."

"And I must say that I was impressed with your counter-surveillance skills," Rawlgeeb replied. "Very effective."

Vince shrugged. "I've figured out a few things. I modified my handset a while back, and once you told me the frequencies to use, it was just a matter of–"

"Yeah, yeah," Brent interrupted. "Listen, now we've shaken our spy in the sky, we need someone to stroll on up to the mayor's office and say hi."

They all stared at him, but Maisie recovered first. "Aren't you coming with us?"

"No, I can't." Brent tugged at his shirt collar. "On the way over here, I recalled a little difference of opinion I had with the mayor."

"You had an argument, so what?" Vince asked. "He's not going to hold that against you."

Brent grimaced. "Yes. Yes, he is. In fact, I can't be anywhere within fifty feet of his office."

"Oh, I see," Maisie put in. "He put a restraining order on you."

Brent tilted his head from side to side. "It was more of an unwritten understanding. The mayor made an emphatic suggestion that I should keep my distance, and I was happy to agree with him as soon as I recovered the power of speech, which, I'm pleased to say, was right after he let go of my throat."

Maisie let out a low whistle. "I'd never have guessed he was like that. On TV, he always seems so nice."

"What can I tell you? Never trust a politician, or, it turns out, a politician's spouse." Brent looked around the group. "Maisie, you're the obvious choice. I think you should go talk to him."

Maisie lifted her left eyebrow. "Why is that? Because I'm pretty? Is that the only way a woman can have power and influence in your book?"

"Not at all," Brent protested. "I just figured that with your work at the UN, you'd be highly skilled in the art of talking to powerful people, that's all."

"Oh." Maisie's cheeks colored slightly. "I see. Yes, well, I suppose you're right."

"Plus, it doesn't hurt that you're easy on the eye," Brent added. "No offense intended, but the mayor is a man with a finely honed appreciation for the female form if you know what I mean."

"I should've known!" Maisie snapped. "I won't be the worm on your hook, Brent, so you can forget it. I would've gone in there, but not now. Go see him yourself. You're the one he wants in his pocket, so I guess that makes you his bitch. How do you like that?"

Brent rocked back on his heels. "Please refrain from using gender-based derogatory remarks. Did I call you a dame or refer to you as dollface? No, I did not. I'm not that kind of detective. I'm a modern man with deep thoughts and feelings and all that other sensitive shit."

Maisie looked skyward for a second, a repressed groan sneaking from between her clenched teeth. "Will someone around here please start making sense? *Who* is going to talk to the mayor?"

"I'll go," Rawlgeeb said. "I know him."

Vince laughed. "Come on, man, that's ridiculous."

"Is it?" Rawlgeeb blinked repeatedly. "I appreciate that we didn't exactly get off on the right foot, Vince, but I'll have you know that in some circles, I was a respected figure. I've worked in Earth Liaison for a long time, and I've met all kinds of influential people. In fact, the mayor is one of the least impressive members of that list." He shot Vince a look. "And don't call me *man*–it isn't accurate, and I don't care for it at all."

Vince held up his hands in surrender. "Sorry, dude, er, I mean, what should I call you?"

"Sir?" Rawlgeeb offered hopefully.

"Okay, let's do this," Brent said firmly. "Rawlgeeb, you rock on up to the office and see if you get through to your old buddy. Tell him we found out about him paying the AGI on my behalf, and let him know I'm real keen to talk in person. Got it?"

"I think I can do better than that," Rawlgeeb said. "I'll get us some answers. And I'll go alone. You three can wait here." He hesitated, looking down at his clothes. "Oh flek. I should've found something decent to wear before we came. I should've insisted."

Brent patted him on the arm. "Don't worry about it. Tell them you're on a pilgrimage or something. They won't question it, trust me. We have no idea about Gloabon religion. It's a complete mystery."

"That's because there isn't one," Rawlgeeb stated. "We don't feel the need."

"Excellent, that's one less person on my Christmas card list," Brent said with a grin. "Now, go to it, my friend. Knock 'em dead." His face fell. "That's just an—"

Rawlgeeb cut him off with an imperious wave. "I know. I'm not a complete imbecile." He rolled his eyes then turned and walked away, his back straight. In a few long strides he was outside the mayor's impressive office, and without looking back, he began to climb the broad flight of stone steps.

"Do you think he'll be all right?" Maisie asked.

"Sure," Brent replied. "He's a high-ranking Gloabon from the Earth Liaison Unit. You heard what he said—he's an important guy."

Vince coughed. "Yeah. At least he *was*. But then he got himself kicked out for some reason." He exchanged a look with Brent. "Why was that, do you think? Only, I'm sure he never got around to telling us what happened."

"Probably just a misunderstanding," Brent said with more conviction than he felt. "You know what Gloabons are like—real sticklers for the rules. He probably just parked in someone else's spot or used the wrong spoon or something." He flashed them a reassuring smile. "Listen, Rawlgeeb walked into that building like he owned the place. He's solid, you'll see. I have every faith in him. Every faith."

"Is this based on your instincts as a detective?" Maisie asked.

"Sure."

Maisie hung her head. "Oh hell. We're screwed."

The entrance to the mayor's office building was protected by a security gate, but Rawlgeeb marched straight toward it, his gaze fixed dead ahead. From the corner of his eyes, he registered a pair of security guards scurrying to meet him, but he did not make eye contact.

"Er, excuse me, sir?" one of them called out. "Can we help you?"

Rawlgeeb looked down his nose at the guard. "Stand aside. I am here on official business on behalf of the Gloabon Government."

The guard licked his lips. "Yes, sir, I'm sure that's all fine, but I'd normally ask to see some ID."

"I am Rawlgeeb from the Earth Liaison Unit, *that* is my ID as you call it."

"Right. Yes. Good." The guard lifted a radio from his belt. "I'm sure that will check out if you give me a minute. We have to confirm that you're on the list before we let you in."

"How dare you doubt me?" Rawlgeeb barked. "Tell me your names. Both of you."

The hapless guard flinched. "I'm Dave Murphy, and this here is Frank Deacon."

Rawlgeeb looked from one guard to the other as though memorizing their faces. "We're very interested in sampling humans that meet certain criteria, and you both look like prime candidates. Naturally, we'll need your immediate families too. All of them. Especially the children. And possibly your pets. Tell me, do you have a dog? Yes, you do. I can smell it on you. That's good. I love dog."

"You mean you like *dogs*," Murphy suggested.

"No, I meant exactly what I said. I love *dog*. Raw is best, especially the eyes."

Murphy swallowed. "Listen, sir, I'm sure we can straighten this out."

"Perhaps," Rawlgeeb said. "If I am able to complete my business with Mayor Enderley in a swift and efficient manner, then I'm sure your names might slip my mind. Do you think we might be able to see a way forward?"

Deacon found his voice. "We could call up to Mayor Enderley and tell him that Rawlgeeb is here."

"Very good," Rawlgeeb said. "And please, open the gate. I am unaccustomed to delay."

"Certainly," Murphy said, hurrying to the control panel. "Deacon, make the call."

As the gate swung open, Rawlgeeb stepped inside, scanning the lobby with a serene expression on his face.

"The Mayor says to go straight up," Deacon said in a rush. "Top floor. I can call the elevator for you if you like."

"That will not be necessary," Rawlgeeb replied, and he headed across the lobby at a calm and measured pace. *I can't believe I just did that!* he thought. *I just broke every rule in the book!* And as he waited for the elevator to arrive, he smiled.

On the top floor, Mayor Enderley was waiting by the elevator doors, a fixed grin on his face and his arm outstretched. "Rawlgeeb! Great to see you again."

"Likewise," Rawlgeeb said, taking the mayor's hand. "Sorry about my garb, by the way. It's…well there's no excuse for it really, but there are lots of reasons."

Enderley waved his protestations aside. "First rule of diplomacy—never judge a person by appearances. I've met plenty of people with sharp suits and dull wits, believe me." He gestured toward an open door. "Please, step inside and we'll talk. My office is always happy to help our Gloabon partners."

"Thank you." Rawlgeeb followed the mayor into a spacious office and looked around, admiring the view from the tall windows. The city's parks had made ideal landing grounds for the first wave of Gloabon ships, and as a result, there was scarcely an untouched green space within the city limits. But of the few trees that had been left standing, almost all could be seen from the mayor's office.

"Sit down and make yourself comfortable," Enderley said, installing himself behind a huge oak desk. "What can I do for you?"

Rawlgeeb sat carefully on a padded chair. He'd never quite trusted Earth furniture. A Gloabon's bones were far denser than a human's, and on several occasions, his weight had proved too much for human-made chairs. But this seat seemed to have been suitably reinforced, and Rawlgeeb relaxed a little. "Mayor Enderley, I've come here today to talk with you about a matter of some sensitivity."

"Go ahead. I'm listening."

"Haha! Very good. You sounded just like him." Rawlgeeb's laughter died on his lips. The mayor was frowning, his nostrils flaring, and it looked as though he was trying to decide whether to be offended or angry. *Idiot!* Rawlgeeb scolded himself. *Humans* do not *all sound the same.* "Sorry, I didn't mean to be disrespectful," he blustered. "Perhaps I should start again."

"Yes," the mayor replied, taking a glance at his watch. "I do have another meeting scheduled, so…"

"Of course." Rawlgeeb took a moment to center himself. "Mayor Enderley, I am carrying out an investigation on behalf of the Gloabon High Command. I can't reveal the nature of my inquiries because they're sensitive, but I have–"

"Aha!" Enderley slapped his palm on his desk. "This is about all the missing people!"

Rawlgeeb stared, his lips moving soundlessly. He'd come to gather information, not to give it away. And while he was still furious at the way he'd been treated by his superiors, some loyalties ran deep. Apart from anything else, he still needed to keep his options open. *There's still a chance I could get reinstated on The Gamulon*, he told himself. *I have to keep a cool head*. He looked down at his hands for a moment and made a show of smoothing the ridiculous pants. "Missing people, Mister Mayor? Whatever gave you that idea?"

"Don't play that game with me. Did you really think we wouldn't notice all those folks disappearing off the face of the Earth? We do have an administration of our own, you know."

"I really can't discuss it," Rawlgeeb said primly. "My lips are sealed."

"Well, I *can!* I've got the police department going crazy, the FBI jumping all over the joint, the CIA coming up with wild theories, the NSA blaming the CIA, the military types slugging it out for extra funding, and meanwhile, the dear old UN is busy arguing about what kind of mineral water to serve when we finally surrender." He paused to glare at Rawlgeeb. "You people have clipped our wings pretty good. There isn't hardly a damned thing down here that doesn't run on Gloabon tech, but you can only push us so far before we start pushing back."

Choose your next words very carefully, Rawlgeeb told himself. *You don't want to go down in history as the Gloabon who started a war*. He licked his lips. "All right. I'll admit it. It's distinctly possible that there is a discrepancy between the number of people who should have been legally sampled and the number who were actually taken."

"Some discrepancy! I'm talking about thousands of people, and that's just from this heap of rock we used to call the USA."

Rawlgeeb sat very still. *Thousands! Why the hell didn't Tsumper tell me that?* But of course, he knew the answer. He'd been used, sent out into a potentially dangerous situation without adequate knowledge: a canary lowered into a coal mine. *Or dropped headfirst into an active volcano*, he thought. He drummed his fingers on the chair's armrests. "I'm sorry, but I don't have the figures to hand."

"Well, what *do* you have?" Enderley demanded. "If I know Gloabons, and I do, you must've come here for *something*. Spit it out."

Rawlgeeb almost smiled, the phrase taking him back to the moment he'd first met Breamell. But he didn't have time for reminiscences; he had a job to do. "I'm following a line of inquiry, looking into what happened to some specific individuals so that I can trace the root of the problem, and that has led me to a man called Brent Bolster."

The mayor sat back, realization dawning. "Ah, about time that guy came into play. I sprung him out when I heard he got snatched. I figured he might be useful."

"How did you find out about that?" Rawlgeeb asked quickly. "That information in itself might be of vital importance. No one's supposed to know when a sample is taken."

"All AGI members have an implant under their skins–a tracking device. They know when one of their own has been taken, and let's just say I have contacts within the AGI. One hand washes the other."

"Yes, I suppose it does," Rawlgeeb said wisely, looking carefully at the mayor's large hands. "That's very…hygienic."

Enderley shook his head. "Forget about it. The point is, where the hell is Bolster? It's been over a week, and the jerk hasn't even called to say thank you."

"He's been missing for ten days," Rawlgeeb replied. "We don't know what happened, but he's helping me with this inquiry, and he's keen to meet with you in person. He's worried that he wouldn't be able to visit this office for…for health reasons."

"Fair enough." Enderley looked thoughtful. "Are you on the level, Rawlgeeb? Are you really trying to find out what's going on, or did they send you down here to cover the whole thing up?"

Rawlgeeb leaned forward. "Believe me, Mayor Enderley, I want to get to the bottom of this, for a number of *very* good reasons."

Enderley studied Rawlgeeb's expression as if playing a hand at poker, then he flashed him a vote-winning smile, at once warm, business-like, and sincere. "Have him meet me at my house tonight. And you come along too."

"Thank you," Rawlgeeb replied. "That would be perfect. And would it be all right if we bring along someone else? There's a woman who was also taken. She works for the UN, so she could be a useful contact."

"Bring who you like. Bring your old maid aunt for all I care, but Rawlgeeb, there's one thing you need to do for me, and I'm deadly serious about this." He locked eyes with Rawlgeeb, and as he did so, he cracked his knuckles, one by one. "Do not turn up at my house in those goddamned rags."

"Yes, of course. But what you said about appearances—"

"That's for business," Enderley interrupted, "but this is my home we're talking about, so get some decent clothes or don't come at all. I have neighbors, for fuck's sake, and I don't want them thinking I've got some kind of weird, hippie, fancy dress party going on." He grimaced. "That kind of thing can get a fella kicked out of the golf club."

"Right," Rawlgeeb said slowly. He stood, still trying to process the mayor's apparently contradictory reasoning. *Why must humans always cling so tightly to their little tribes?* he wondered. *And the funny thing is, they never seem to realize they're doing it.* But aloud, he simply said, "Would eight o'clock be a suitable time?"

"It's a date," Enderley said, already lifting his handset and tapping the screen. "A secretary will show you out."

"No need." Rawlgeeb made for the door and let himself out, heading for the elevator. He had a lot to tell Brent and the others, and he had a feeling they'd be pleased.

CHAPTER 16

Aboard *The Kreltonian Skull* - Andromeda Class Battle Cruiser.

Official Status: Missing Presumed Destroyed.

Ship's Log: Earth Orbit.

In his executive office, Admiral Norph drummed his talons on the metal workstation and glared at the blank screen. "Late," he muttered. "Typical. Bloody Gloabons. Alien scum."

He made to stand, ready to walk away, but before he could get to his feet, the screen flickered into life, and Norph accepted the incoming call, hitting the button so hard his talon dented its reinforced alloy casing. "What took you so long?"

The dark figure on the screen tilted its head, its features lost in the shadows. "I called at the appointed hour, precisely as arranged. Any error must be yours."

Norph glanced at the time displayed on the top-right corner of his screen. Since changing the ship's clocks over to Standard Andelian Time, he'd missed breakfast in the galley twice and arrived for dinner far too early on three separate occasions, but he'd be damned before he'd change the clocks back to the ridiculous Kreitian system; it was a matter of principle. Also, his missed meals had provided him excellent opportunities for flogging the galley staff, so it hadn't all been bad. Perhaps, when all this was over, he'd be able to get his hands on his impudent Gloabon contact and show him how an Andelian dealt with such flagrant disrespect. But for now, he must satisfy himself with the knowledge that one day soon, his enemies would suffer. All of them.

Norph scowled at the screen. "Don't push your luck. Just

give me a progress report and keep it short. I'm hungry." He bared his teeth. "How goes our great project?"

"On schedule, of course." The Gloabon paused. "Is there any other way?"

Norph chuckled darkly. "Excellent. My ship has remained cloaked since we dropped out of warp. We're certain your space station has not detected us, but can you confirm that?"

"Definitely. I'd have known immediately if your vessel had been spotted"

Norph grinned. "And what about the humans–do they suspect anything?"

"There have been *rumblings,* but it's nothing I can't contain." The figure hesitated. "I'm more concerned about the Gloabon High Command. Something's going on there, but I haven't been able to get to the bottom of it."

"I don't like the sound of that," Norph muttered. "Nevertheless, I need the details. What's the problem?"

"The High Command has discovered the discrepancies in our records, and they have demanded an investigation. Fortunately, I was able to use my influence to hamper their activities."

"How so?"

"I helped to select the officer in charge of the inquiry. I made sure they picked a no-hoper, a young commander with lots of ambition but no experience of intelligence work whatsoever. Tsumper is her name, and she'll get nowhere, mark my words." The Gloabon laughed quietly.

"None of this strikes me as funny," Norph snarled. "She could ruin everything."

"Sorry, but I had to laugh. She's cooked up some harebrained scheme and roped in the most incompetent buffoon you've ever seen." He chortled under his breath. "She even staged a fake banishment, but I saw through it immediately. It was really quite comical. Her poor stooge got beaten up and exiled for no good reason at all."

Norph joined in the laughter. "Really? They beat him? His own people?" He thumped the workstation with his fists in excitement. "Wonderful. I like it. Did they beat his brains out? Did they kill him? Did they?"

The Gloabon stopped laughing abruptly. "No. That would've been pointless. She wants to use him. Don't you understand?"

"Don't patronize me," Norph snapped. "Of course I understand. I'm not some dumb animal and don't you forget it. You'll see what I'm capable of when we put phase two into operation."

"Actually, we've already completed phases two through four. We're in phase five at the moment, so the next stage will be phase six."

Norph narrowed his eyes. "Six, seven, it doesn't matter. Call it what you wish, the humans will still be dealt with, and then we shall claim the planet for Free Andel, making it a new homeland for all those who wish to escape the oppression of the Kreitian tyrants."

"We shall claim Earth *together*," the Gloabon said frostily. "Do not forget our agreement, Admiral. You may settle as many of your people on Earth as you wish, but the Gloabons will retain administrative control under *my* command."

"Yes, yes. It's understood. All true Andelians are warriors. We care nothing for your petty rules and regulations. We'll gladly leave that nonsense to you and your army of spineless, pencil-necked pen-pushers. Ha!" Norph grinned, picturing the heel of his boot pressing down on the long neck of his Gloabon contact.

On the screen, the dark figure stirred as though agitated, and when he spoke again, his voice was pure ice. "On Earth, they have a saying–the pen is mightier than the sword. Perhaps there will come a time to test the validity of that statement."

"I know where I'd put my faith. Give me a sword anytime. I once had to eviscerate an ensign with a pen, and it took hours. They were good hours, mind, but even so…" Norph sat back, scratching at his belly. "All these reminiscences are making me hungry. I'm going to eat. We'll talk soon. In the meantime, keep me informed. Norph out." He terminated the call and pushed himself up from his chair, heading for the door. He entered the bridge but kept walking, ducking into the elevator and hitting the button for level B three. Humming a tuneless rhythm, he watched the display count down the levels. The elevator halted on level one, and Norph frowned at the display while jabbing the button for B three repeatedly. But despite his efforts, the doors hummed open, revealing a single member of the crew. But no. This was no true Andelian.

Norph glared. "Zak3? You damned android! I thought I'd got rid of you for good." He drew his bolt gun. "I can't believe I have to do this again. I hate to repeat myself." He leveled his weapon, but unperturbed, the cybonic lifeform stepped into the elevator, the doors hissing closed behind him.

"My name is Zeb," he said, selecting a floor from the control panel. "I'm sorry, but if you seek an android named Zak3, I'm not the droid you're looking for."

"Wait a minute!" Norph growled as the elevator hummed into motion. "Something's going on here. All right, so you're not Zak3, any fool can see that. But who the hell are you? And what are you doing on my ship?"

Zeb dipped his chin. "I am the new science officer, and I have just been activated." He glanced at the bolt gun in Norph's hand. "Also, taking current circumstances into account, I am delighted to report that I have no knowledge of Zak3 whatsoever, nor do I know what happened to him."

Norph moved a little closer to him. "If you're really the science officer, why haven't you reported to the bridge? What are you doing skulking around down here?"

"Completing my induction program," Zeb said smoothly. "All new personnel must complete a number of mandatory training and orientation sessions. At present, I am touring the ship, ensuring that I am familiar with its layout and specifications."

The lift halted, and Zeb checked the display as the doors slid open. "This is my floor. I must now tour the weapon storage bay and the torpedo rooms. Good day, Admiral." He made for the doorway, but at the last second, Norph grabbed him by the upper arm, his talons sinking deep into Zeb's sturdy frame.

"You want a tour of the ship?" Norph asked, his voice dangerously quiet. "I'll show you something you won't find on the blueprints."

Zeb looked down at him. "With all due respect, that seems unlikely, Admiral. The schematic diagrams are–"

"Silence!" Norph interrupted, punching the button to close the elevator doors. "I'll show you something *special*, and then we'll see what you're made of, my metallic friend. Then we'll see whose side you're on."

"Of course." Zeb offered a strained smile as the elevator resumed its journey. "Naturally, I shall be pleased to carry out any legal order."

"Legal order?" Norph's jaw worked soundlessly as if he were struggling to speak in some strange new language. "Are you deliberately testing my patience? I *am* the law on board this ship. If I give an order, that makes it legal. End of story." The admiral waved his weapon in the air for added emphasis. "Do you understand?"

Zeb's eyes followed the bolt gun's path. "Yes, Admiral. I agree. One hundred percent, sir." Then, as if speaking to himself, he murmured, "Heck, this is easier than I thought."

Norph narrowed his eyes, but before he could speak again, the elevator halted.

"We have arrived at level B three," Zeb said. "This area contains recycling facilities, storage bays, and the waste processing plant."

Norph grunted and gestured toward the doors as they opened. "Move. Get out then turn right. Keep walking until I say stop."

"Understood." Zeb headed out through the doors and did as he was told, taking long strides, his footsteps thudding on the metal walkway, the rhythm reverberating along the empty corridor.

"Stop!" Norph said, and Zeb halted beside a large, heavily reinforced door. Holstering his gun, Norph placed his hand on the door's touch panel, and somewhere within the wall, a hollow clunk rang out. Motors droned, and with a muffled hiss, the door swung slowly open, releasing a cloud of swirling mist. "Inside," Norph snapped.

Zeb hesitated. "Sir, my sensors indicate an extremely low temperature within that storage bay. It would be damaging to both of us, and I advise you against stepping inside."

"You know the problem with you damned robots?" Norph asked. "You talk too much." He put his hand in the small of Zeb's back and shoved. Hard. Caught off-guard, Zeb stumbled forward, his momentum taking him inside the storage bay. He regained his balance, and as he turned around, Admiral Norph stood in the doorway, his squat figure blocking the only exit. "I usually have to fetch my own snacks," Norph began, "but since you're here, you may as well make yourself useful."

"Sir, this temperature is affecting my sen…sen…sen." Zeb shuddered. "I'm too cold. It's hurting my head."

Norph waved airily. "Any one of them will do. No, make it a large one. And quick about it. I'm starving."

"Sir, I don't…" The clouds of mist cleared, and Zeb's words died on his lips. "Sir, this is…this is…"

"My meat locker," Norph said, licking his lips. "Get that one on the right. And be quick about it. I'm freezing my ass off here."

As if in a trance, Zeb crossed the vast storage bay, staring at the huge racks that ran along both sides, each one packed with row upon row of transparent body bags. "There are hundreds," he murmured. "Thousands." He glanced back at Norph. "And I'm picking up life signs. Unless the cold is affecting my sensors, these beings are…they're still alive."

"What do you expect?" Norph snorted. "A good Andelian does not eat dead meat, but as in the ancient legends, he feasts on the flesh and bones of his enemies while the blood still flows within their bodies." He bared his teeth and raised his arms, his expansive gesture taking in the whole of the vast cavern, and Zeb looked on in mute horror. The bay's walls dwindled away into the mist in the distance, the crowded racks defeating Zeb's tenuous grasp of reality.

"So what do you think of my little larder?" Norph went on. "Is it not a marvel of the modern age? Can you begin to comprehend how this place will be the start of it all? This is just the beginning. From here on in, this ship, *our* ship, will be the bringer of a new dawn. We shall be heralded as heroes, fearless leaders in the brave new world of the Second Andelian Empire. Do you not see?"

"Yes," Zeb said, his voice seeming small and distant in the huge chamber. "I understand exactly what you're doing here, Admiral. But the Andel-Kreit coalition is not at war with Earth. And these people are not your enemies–they are humans."

Norph stormed toward him, his face twisted in rage. "I knew it! Another weakling. A traitor to the cause." He snatched a body bag from the nearest rack, slinging it over his shoulder, then he headed for the exit, the body of the unconscious human bouncing and swaying in time with Norph's powerful strides.

"Sir, wait!" Zeb hurried after Norph, but the admiral reached the door first, and stepping smartly outside, he fixed Zeb with a steely smile and reached for the door's control panel.

"Goodbye," Norph said, and the door swung shut, sealing itself with a resounding thud. The admiral chuckled under his breath. The dumb robot had looked hilarious as it had thrown itself at the door. It was almost as if it were possessed of the desire to live, to preserve itself. "Ridiculous!" Norph muttered, then he marched away, heading for the elevator. If he was lucky, he'd have no interruptions on the way back to his quarters. And if he was really lucky, he'd arrive at his stateroom just as his snack was defrosting. *Starting to struggle but not quite ready to put up a full-blown fight,* he thought. *Medium-rare, just the way I like it.*

CHAPTER 17

Earth

Brent stared out the side window of the cut-price robocab. *I'd rather have walked*, he thought, but Maisie had insisted they take a cab, and now they were trapped in the cramped, driverless vehicle. Brent was pressed against one door by Vince's bulk while Rawlgeeb had somehow managed to concertina himself into what space remained on the stained and torn vinyl of the narrow backseat. Maisie rode up front, but since she'd agreed to pay the fare, there'd been no way for Brent to argue over the seating allocation.

"Here we go again," Vince moaned. "Could this thing have *found* a longer route to the mayor's house?"

Rawlgeeb muttered something wearily under his breath, and Brent thought it sounded like, "Friends", but he'd learned not to ask the Gloabon for explanations; they made Brent want to drain a bottle of whiskey down his gullet, not least so he'd have an empty vessel to break over the alien's head.

The cab slowed for the seventh time as it passed a restaurant, and the rear windows rolled down. "Fresh pizza," a recorded voice intoned. "Hand-stretched by the finest Italian robots, our pizza bases are delicious. Top it with your favorite synthetic meats, vegetable substitutes, or cheese flavored algae. Yum!"

"No!" Maisie snapped. "Just take us where we want to go."

The cab picked up speed, the windows closing. "Thank you for considering our sponsors," the recording droned. "In order to provide you with services that may interest you, we have scanned the financial details of all occupants and cross-referenced your purchase histories with your socio-economic profiles. Based on your data, we think you'd like to call in at…Mistress Naughty's Sexy Times Emporium."

In the tense silence, the occupants of the backseat eyed each other suspiciously. Maisie did not turn around. "No thank you," she said tartly. "Can't we just opt out of all these advertisements and detours? I'll happily pay extra."

"Thank you," the voice murmured. "We take your privacy seriously. To opt out of sponsored opportunities, visit our website, create an account and update your preferences, confirming your choices by uploading your government ID, completing a retinal scan, and submitting a sample of saliva. Meanwhile, how about a fresh cup of coffee?"

The cab slowed, and Rawlgeeb, who'd been strangely reticent until this point, slammed his fist against the car door. "No! We do not want anything! Drive!"

Brent closed his eyes and tuned out the sound as the recorded message started up again. It had been one hell of a day, and if nothing else, the back of the cab was warm. He needed to be ready for action, but it was okay to rest his eyelids for a moment because, with one thing and another, there was no way he could fall asleep. No way whatsoever.

***

"Wake up, we're here."

Someone nudged Brent's arm, and he opened his eyes with a start. "I wasn't asleep," he spluttered, wiping his mouth with the back of his hand.

"Right, Mr. Drool," Vince said. "Just open the door, will you?"

"Yeah yeah." Brent pushed the door open and climbed out, arching his back and feeling the vertebrae click into something like their allotted positions.

Maisie stood at his side. "Nice place, huh?"

Brent grunted. "Always nice to see my tax credits at work." He let his eyes roam over the impressive facade of what could only be described as a mansion.

"You pay taxes?" Maisie regarded him with a smirk, her eyebrows raised.

"Once," Brent admitted. "That's two and a half credits I'll never see again." He grinned. "I got my own back though. When I called in at the tax office to pay the bill, I stole a pen from the counter. Chain and all."

"I always wondered what kind of schmuck stole those," Maisie said. "And now that I know, I can't honestly say I'm surprised."

"Well, the government may have spent my credits in a second," Brent said, "but I have that pen to this day, and it still works too. Almost all of the time."

Maisie sighed and looked back at the cab where Vince and Rawlgeeb were having difficulty extricating themselves from the backseat. "Should we help them?"

"Nah. Let them figure it out." Brent suppressed a chuckle as Rawlgeeb accidentally elbowed Vince in the eye. "Think of it as a team-building exercise," Brent added. "Co-operation and problem-solving. Good for morale."

Maisie didn't look convinced, but Vince and Rawlgeeb were finally working together, and they completed their undignified exit from the cab without further injury. As the vehicle drove away, the pair stood beside Brent, both wearing pained expressions. "I cricked my neck," Vince complained. "I can't turn my head."

"Think yourself lucky," Rawlgeeb chipped in. "I've lost all circulation to my–" he stopped abruptly. "Never mind."

Brent looked Rawlgeeb up and down, but as fast as questions sprang into his mind, he pushed them aside. There were some things that he really did not want to know; not at any price.

"At least the two of you look the part now," Maisie said brightly. "Much better."

Rawlgeeb stood a little taller, smoothing down his brand new jumpsuit. "Yes, thank you, Ms. Richmond. I shall, of course, repay you as soon as I can."

"Yeah, and thanks for having my jacket fixed," Vince put in. "That was real kind of you. And this trench coat…well, it's just awesome. I'll send you the money when we get back to town."

Maisie smiled graciously. "No problem. And please don't worry about the coat, Vince. Consider it a gift. Not only does it make you look like an investigator, but it also covers up your, er, delightful jacket." She gestured toward the mansion's imposing front door. "Shall we?"

"Let's go," Brent said, and he led the way along the broad, graveled path, the others following close behind.

Brent pointed upward. "The towers are a nice touch. Real homey."

"Equipped with automated sentry guns," Vince put in. "It's a damned good thing he's expecting us, otherwise we'd have been cut to pieces by now."

"Seriously?" Maisie asked.

"I'd say that our mayor is a man who takes his privacy seriously," Brent said. "And since he's invited us into his castle, you can bet that whatever he's got to tell us, it has to be big."

They walked on in silence, and as they neared the door, it swung open, a robotic servant standing politely to one side. "Please, step this way," it said. "My name is Bartleby, Mayor Enderley's butler. The mayor is waiting for you in the conservatory."

"Neat," Brent said as he walked inside, then he turned to Maisie, and from the corner of his mouth asked, "A conservatory? I thought that was like a fancy music school or something."

Maisie rolled her eyes. "You really are a dinosaur, aren't you, Brent?"

Brent shrugged. "Better a dinosaur than, er, some other thing…" His voice trailed away as he watched Maisie hand her coat to Bartleby. She'd come dressed to impress, and her gown, cut from a seamless, skin-tight fabric, was a subtle shade of deep scarlet, the plunging neckline apparently designed to cause the higher functioning chunks of Brent's gray matter to short-circuit, while the more basic components of his central nervous system chose this moment to send his cardiovascular system into overdrive. At times like this, he knew that it was better if he said nothing at all, but despite his best efforts, a single whispered word slipped from his slack-jawed mouth: "Wow!"

"What's the matter, Brent?" Maisie asked. "Cat got your tongue?"

Brent clamped his lips firmly together and turned away, pushing his hands deep into his pockets as he started walking, heading for the nearest open door. "Come on, you rabble. Keep up. We're here on business."

"Sir!" Bartleby called out. "You're going the wrong way."

Brent stopped dead in the doorway and stared into the huge room beyond, taking in its air of restrained grandeur. A polished wooden table ran the length of the room with places already set for dinner. Brent guessed there were at least thirty sets of glittering silverware and gleaming glasses, and the elaborate centerpieces ranged down the startlingly white linen runner showed that a special occasion was to be celebrated. But his eyes lingered on an elegant cage set at one end of the table. The cage was of a type that might have held a parrot or similar large bird, but from within the thin metal bars, a large iguana stared out, blinking in the room's bright lights.

Brent sensed the butler standing close behind him, and he turned to face the mechanical servant. "I was just checking around. I see you're expecting guests. Gloabons too. My invite seems to have got lost in the mail."

Bartleby tilted its head. "Yes, the mayor is hosting an important dinner tonight, and so time is pressing. Please, allow me to show you to the conservatory." He stood waiting, his arm extended toward the entrance hall.

Brent shrugged. "Go for it, Beetlebum. Right behind you."

Somewhat uncertainly, the butler performed a small bow, then it set off at a brisk pace, Brent and the others trailing in its wake.

They followed the butler down the richly carpeted hallway and into a wide room, its ceiling and outer walls made from curved glass panels that afforded a grand view over the city's twinkling lights. Mayor Enderley was wearing a brown smock and tending to a pot plant, fussing over its foliage with gloved hands, but he looked up as they walked in, laying down the stout pair of scissors he'd been using to snip back the plant's creeping tendrils. "Thank you, Bartleby," he said. "Leave us now."

Bartleby bowed low. "Very good, sir. May I remind you

that your guests will arrive in thirty minutes?"

"Sure, sure." Enderley removed his heavy-duty gloves and looked fondly at the newly trimmed plant. "Carnivorous orchids. They're a passion of mine. Very hard to keep alive. And if you don't know what you're doing, they'll give you bite that'll make your eyes water."

"Andelian blood blossom," Maisie said knowledgeably. "I didn't think they were allowed on Earth."

Enderley shrugged. "These specimens are only hybrids, so legally, it's a gray area. I'd love to have the real thing, but it was hard enough to get these beauties imported. Fortunately, I know the right people, but I won't bore you with the details." He removed his smock, pulling it over his head and then hanging the strangely stiff garment from a hook on the wall. "This damned thing weighs a ton. Lined with metal plates. Only thing that stops them. But you didn't come here to talk about horticulture."

"Ooh, I know a joke about that," Rawlgeeb chipped in. Dorothy Parker said, "You can take…"

"Let's not lower the tone," Brent said quickly, glancing at Maisie. "Not the time, Rawlgeeb, and definitely not the place." He stepped closer to the mayor. "I really appreciate you seeing us at such short notice. I hope that we can put the past behind us and work together to clear up this situation."

Enderley pursed his lips. "Possibly. Listen, don't take this personally, Brent, because I know you investigators can be brittle about these things."

"Brittle?" Brent snapped. "Who the hell are you calling brittle?"

"See what I mean?" Enderley shook his head, chortling

to himself. "It's like this, Brent: I've known about the missing people for quite a while now, and any fool could see that the authorities on Earth were getting nowhere. I knew I needed a private investigator, but you weren't exactly my first choice."

Brent nodded. "That's no problem. Some people don't like to play second fiddle, but I don't give a damn so long as the money's there. What happened to your first guy—couldn't cut it, huh?"

Enderley looked pained. "Let me show you something." He led them over to a glass door and threw it wide open. Automatic floodlights flared into life, and squinting against the glare, Brent took in the broad sweep of a paved terrace that led up a gentle slope and toward a large pool. There was nothing remarkable on the terrace; just the usual scattering of poolside tables and chairs punctuated by potted palms. But the pool was a different matter. The angle prevented Brent from seeing down into the water, but just visible above the pool's lip, a dark shape bobbed gently up and down.

"The man you can see over there," Enderley went on, "is the thirty-fifth investigator I hired. And I found him sort of floating around in there this morning."

Maisie gasped. "Didn't you call the police?"

"Oh, he's not dead," Enderley said. "Dawson, say hi to my guests."

The man in the pool raised an arm and waved. "Hello there," he called out, his English accent unmistakable. "Lovely evening, isn't it?"

"Whoever I hire, something weird always happens to them," Enderley explained. "I don't know if you can do any better, but I can't keep on hiring people and then losing them in bizarre ways."

"What's so bizarre about this guy?" Vince asked. "I mean, he didn't even take his clothes off before he dived in, but hell, we've all done that when we've had too many drinks, right?"

Enderley stared at Vince. "You're an idiot, aren't you? I guess Brent keeps you around for muscle, but even so..." He rubbed his hand across his forehead.

"That's not very nice," Vince began, but Brent hinted he should keep quiet by the subtle application of his elbow to Vince's ribcage.

"In case you hadn't noticed," Enderley said with exaggerated patience, "there is no water in the goddamned pool. We drained it for repairs last week."

Maisie was the first to recover her wits. "So, what's keeping him up?"

"We don't know," Enderley replied. "Whatever it is, we can't get near him. Our best guess is that it's some kind of force field. Maybe Gloabon tech." He threw Rawlgeeb a meaningful look.

Brent stroked his chin. "I see the problem. The guy's English, right?"

Enderley nodded. "I had him flown here especially. He had a slick operation over there, running a whole bunch of stuff from the South-East Crater. You know, where London used to be."

"There you go then," Brent announced. "Problem solved. Those English guys are always acting like they're above everyone else. Looks like it finally came true."

"Are you for real?" Enderley looked down at the ground, wringing his hands together. "My God, I knew I was scraping the bottom of the barrel, but this..."

"If I might interject," Rawlgeeb put in. "Perhaps we might glean some useful information from a closer inspection."

"Maybe," Enderley replied without looking up, "but I already have a guy working to get him down from there." He trudged over to the pool's edge. "Hey, Doc. Climb up out of there and tell us what's going on."

A crackling sound split the air and a flash of brilliant, blue light flew up from the pool. Someone let out a yelp, then a tremulous voice called out, a hint of desperation in its tone: "I'll be right there, Mayor. I just…I just have to put this fire out."

Enderley managed a humorless smile. "Never seen anyone set themselves alight in a pool before. Maybe we should just let the water back in and see what happens."

A thin, gangling man clambered from the pool, clouds of smoke still trailing from his white lab coat. "No, don't do that. Please. I have a lot of *very* valuable equipment down there, and it would be ruined. *Ruined*."

"Relax, doc," Enderley said. "Just tell us when we can get Dawson out of there. He's still charging me a grand a day, and he ain't exactly getting results while he's stuck in midair."

"Certainly." The thin man finished flapping at his lab coat and walked toward Brent and the others, his arm extended for a shake. "My name's Doctor Cooper. I work for the Gloabon Institute of Technology, but I've been asked to come over here and help the mayor with his little problem."

"You're with GIT," Brent said, shaking his hand. "Impressive."

The doctor grinned, his smile just a little too wide. "I don't usually get out of the lab much. Fieldwork isn't really my area, but the mayor is very, er, very persuasive." He glanced quickly over his shoulder. "Unfortunately, I'm not really making any progress with this case. The technology behind this force field is like nothing I've ever encountered."

"Force fields are commonplace on Gloabon vessels," Rawlgeeb offered.

"Yes, but they're not like this one," Cooper insisted. "The frequencies are all wrong for Gloabon field generators. And anyway, this isn't a defensive field. It's more like…more like it's been *weaponized*."

"Dawson didn't start off in the pool," Enderley explained. "He was out front, coming over here to give me his report, and the next thing he knew, he was blasted clean off the sidewalk. Flew clean over the house and landed right there."

"I am still here, you know," Dawson called out. "It's terribly rude to chinwag about a chap while he's still within earshot if you ask me."

"That's terrible," Vince said. "The guy's mind is totally scrambled. I could hardly understand a word of what he just said."

"That's just how they talk over there," Rawlgeeb explained. "Believe me, he's a lot easier to understand than Daphne's brothers."

"Daphne?" Enderley asked. "Who the hell is Daphne?" He looked at Maisie. "Are *you* Daphne?"

"No," Maisie said. "Listen, we're getting sidetracked. Mr. Dawson, what can you tell us about the attack?"

"Not a thing, old girl," Dawson replied. "And before you ask, I can't remember anything about my investigation either. It's all gone. It's as if my memory has been wiped. I can recall the flight from England–I had a really awful cup of tea on the plane–but after that, it's all a complete blank."

"Okay, so he must have found something out, and someone wanted him stopped." Maisie turned to Cooper. "Doctor, if the weapon used wasn't Gloabon tech, then where did it come from?"

The doctor pushed out his lower lip. "I'm really not certain."

"Give us your best guess," Maisie insisted. "You must have some idea."

"All right." Cooper hesitated. "It has all the hallmarks of an Andelian weapon."

"Hold on a minute," Enderley said. "Just be careful. The Andelians haven't set foot on Earth, and so long as we can rely on our Gloabon friends, that's the way it stays. But if people think those bloodsuckers have been taking potshots at the mayor's house…" He held out his hands as if the conclusion were self-evident.

"There could be a degree of panic," Rawlgeeb offered, "both on Earth and within the Gloabon High Command."

Enderley nodded. "Exactly. We don't want to start any rumors. Brent, you can have a free hand in this investigation, provided you don't breathe a word to anyone about any possible involvement of the Andelians. Not one word, understand?"

"Agreed," Brent replied. "I'll take the case, but you need to send me all the data you have on these missing people. And I mean all of it. If it turns out you've been holding out on me, the deal's off."

"Consider it done," Enderley said. "I keep all the data stored in an encrypted vault. I'll have the access details sent to your account. Anything else you need, just call my office."

"How about a ride back to town," Brent suggested. "The

147

sooner we get back to base, the sooner I can get started."

"The sooner *we* can get started," Rawlgeeb corrected him.

"I'll send a car around front for you." Enderley looked around the group expectantly. "Is that it?"

Maisie pointed at Doctor Cooper. "I want him."

Doctor Cooper sagged visibly. His complexion, already pale, passed through sickly to anemic, paused briefly at ashen, and then settled on a ghastly shade of fish-belly white. "Me? You want me? Well, I'm very flattered and everything, but I'm not sure whether we'd be, erm, compatible. You see, I still live with my mother, and…"

"For God's sake, put him out of his misery," Brent muttered.

Maisie sighed. "Doctor Cooper, I was simply requesting your assistance in your capacity as a man of science. It strikes me, that as an expert in the field of alien tech, you'd be an ideal person to help us with our investigation."

"Oh, that's different." Cooper's cheeks colored just enough to make him look alive. "I suppose I could help. That's if the mayor can spare me, of course."

Enderley waved him away. "Go. You may as well. You're getting no results with Dawson. Maybe, if you can figure out who zapped him, we can get him out of there."

"Don't mind me," Dawson yelled. "I'm fine here, floating in midair. Really, just ignore me completely, why don't you?"

"There we are," Enderley said. "Everybody's happy."

"I think Dawson's just being passive-aggressive," Rawlgeeb suggested. "They do that a lot in England."

"Who cares? Take the doc, and bring him back when all this makes sense. Or something like sense–I'm not fussy.

Let's face it, either way, I'll be looking to write the whole thing off against taxes." Enderley smiled. "But listen, do your best, Brent. I want this whole thing ironed out."

"Protecting the electorate, huh?" Brent drawled.

"Yeah," Enderley replied. "Plus, I really need to get my pool back."

CHAPTER 18

Earth

Back in Brent's office, the team arranged themselves around the room. Brent perched on the edge of his desk, deep in thought. Vince offered Maisie the chair reserved for clients, and while she sat down, he retreated to his desk and busied himself with his laptop. Rawlgeeb stepped toward Brent as if hoping to join him, but when he caught Brent's expression, he changed his mind and made for the side of the room where he leaned against the filing cabinet. The Gloabon grimaced, examining Algernon with suspicion, then he folded his long arms and stood in silence. Doctor Cooper, meanwhile, hunched in the corner, fussing over the apparatus they'd brought over from the mayor's house. They'd all helped to lug the heavy machinery up the stairs, but despite Cooper's entreaties for them to take care, there'd been more than one unfortunate incident during the climb up the narrow stairway. Cooper tutted as he brushed traces of plaster from a machine, then he cast a furtive irate glance at Brent and the others.

Brent looked away. No one had admitted responsibility, but he knew that most of the machines bore scuff marks and dents that hadn't been there before. It was tough on the doc, but it was just too damned bad. *We don't have time to sweat the small stuff,* he told himself. *We have to kick this investigation into gear. I need to take control of this rag-tag mob or we'll be dead in the water.* He ran through a few opening lines in his mind, but none of them fitted the bill, and he'd be damned if he was going to be the first to say something trivial or just plain stupid. Unfortunately, it looked as though the others had reached the same conclusion, and apart from Rawlgeeb and Algernon, they were all doing their best to avoid any kind of eye contact. An oppressive silence filled the room, its tyranny disturbed only by the gentle rhythm of Vince's fingers on his keyboard.

So when the large, white envelope slid under the door, they all jumped.

Vince raced to the door, yanking it open and disappearing outside.

"You're wasting your time," Brent called after him, and sure enough, when Vince returned a moment later, he was downcast.

"Did you see anyone?" Maisie asked.

Vince shook his head. "No. There's no one there."

"I told you so," Brent said, striding across the room and scooping up the envelope. "It's the way these things are done. It doesn't matter where you are or what time of day or night it happens. The envelope slides through, you dash to the door, no one there. It never changes."

"That doesn't make any kind of sense," Maisie objected. "Vince was only a second. Whoever was out there, they didn't have time to get away."

Brent shrugged. "Hey, I don't make the rules."

"Fascinating!" Cooper blurted out. He stood slowly, his eyes alight with excitement. "If it's as you say, and the phenomenon recurs every time, perhaps there are disruptions in the space-time continuum. There could be rifts in the fabric of space-time. Or in this case, there could be a localized temporal dilation in your hallway. A vortex perhaps."

"No, I'm afraid not," Brent assured him. "It's just that the people who do these things are always, and without exception, sneaky little bastards." He tore open the envelope and drew out a large photograph. "Just as I thought. Black and white. Eight by ten. Glossy finish. Always the same."

Maisie went to his side and studied the image. "A Gloabon. I wonder who she is."

"What's that?" Rawlgeeb moved with surprising speed, crossing the room and plucking the photo from Brent's fingers. "Oh no! It can't be."

Brent and Maisie exchanged a look. "You know her?" Maisie asked.

Rawlgeeb nodded, his eyes on the photo. "Her name is Breamell. She's…a friend." His hand trembled as he passed the photo back to Brent. "Why? She's got nothing to do with any of this. She's an innocent bystander. How could anyone do that to her?"

Vince peered over Brent's shoulder. "They have her tied up pretty well. Looks like a professional job."

"You might be right," Brent said. "There's a certain style to the way it was done. The perpetrator used some kind of old-fashioned rope, not zip ties or plastic tape. And they've been careful with the background–no details to give away where she might be. Nothing but shadows."

"This is just awful," Maisie breathed. "And I can't believe you're discussing it calmly. We have to help this poor girl. We have to *do* something."

Cooper cleared his throat. "Excuse me, but there appears to be some text on the back of the image. That might be a good place to start."

"Don't try to tell me my job," Brent snapped. "Of course there's writing on the back. There always is. I was just getting to that part." Glaring at Cooper, he flipped the photo over. "If you want to see her alive, meet me at midnight tonight," Brent read. "Come to space dock seven, pier twelve, bay three. I will speak only with Rawlgeeb. He must approach me alone. If you inform the authorities, Breamell will die."

Rawlgeeb stood tall. "I'll do it. I'll go alone. There's no need to involve any of you. Leave it to me–I'll handle it myself." He looked around the group. "Hang on a second. Just to be clear, isn't anyone going to argue with me?"

They all started talking at once.

"Stop!" Maisie called out, holding up her hands for silence. "Thank you." She lowered her hands and looked Rawlgeeb in the eye. "There's no question of you dealing with this on your own. We're going to help you. There's no doubt about that. We wouldn't have it any other way."

"That's right," Brent put in. "We'll stick together. Besides, this has got to be connected to our case, right? If we can nab this kidnapper, we'll get another piece of the puzzle."

Rawlgeeb let out a long breath. "Thank goodness for that. For a second there, I thought I might have to face the assassin alone."

Brent stared at Rawlgeeb. "Assassin! Who said anything about an assassin?"

"Isn't it obvious?" Rawlgeeb asked, pointing to the photograph. "Look at the bindings. Those cords are woven from strips of snarkle skin. Such things are only used by the Gloabon Guild of Assassins."

"Oh boy!" Cooper moaned. "I've heard about them. They're invincible."

Brent scanned the faces of the cobbled-together team, taking in the fear and doubt in their eyes. There was a certain type of significant moment that Brent had learned to recognize over the years: sensitive situations where subtle tactics and delicate diplomacy were required. And he knew exactly how to respond. "Listen, this assassin is not invincible," he cried out, his voice filled with passion. "I don't care what fancy guild he snuck into, he's a Gloabon, just like our good friend, Rawlgeeb. So we know this kidnapper has an ass, all we have to decide is how hard to kick it. Are you with me?"

"Hell yeah!" Vince cried, punching the air. "We are ready to rock!"

Encouraged, Brent stood tall, his chin jutting forward as he addressed his troops. "Vince, you're in charge of surveillance. You've got until midnight to hack into every CCTV camera in dock seven. I want to see every damned square inch of the place in glorious technicolor."

"No problem," Vince replied. "It's just a damned shame I can't hijack the UN drones anymore. They upgraded the encryption with Gloabon tech, and it's impossible to break."

"I can't help you with the UN drones," Rawlgeeb said. "But *The Gamulon* always has plenty of drones in the space docks. Would it help if I could get you control of some of those?"

Vince's mouth hung open for a moment. "You can do that?"

"Certainly. In liaison, we often used drones to track our, er, subjects." Rawlgeeb flinched under the ferocity of Maisie's glare. "But let's not dwell on the past. The point is, I can get you control of several drones. I know all the standard access codes. I have them memorized."

"Excellent," Brent said. "Doc, we could sure use some of your technical know-how. Any of that gear good for tracking Gloabons?"

Cooper nodded reluctantly. "Yes, that's pretty much what it's for. It can pick up the signatures from all kinds of alien tech. I could show you how to use it, then I could stay here by the phone in case you needed technical support."

Brent slapped Cooper on the shoulder. "Forget it, Doc. You're coming along with us. We need you with us. We'll pack up your gear and get a shuttle booked to take us up to the dock." He looked at Maisie, his lips pursed. "You know what I'm thinking?"

"Regrettably, I have that misfortune pretty much all of the time," Maisie replied. "But in this case, I suspect we're both wondering if my contacts at the UN might come in handy. The space docks are under their jurisdiction."

"Exactly," Brent said. "That's precisely what I was thinking, and I was not, under any circumstances, planning to use you as some sort of bait to distract the bad guy."

Maisie lowered her eyebrows. "And what about you, Brent? What are *you* going to do?"

"Me? I'm going to do what I do best."

"And that is?" Maisie queried. "I ask merely for information."

Brent grinned. "If you want to catch a devious bastard, you set another devious bastard on his tail."

"You have absolutely no idea what you're going to do, have you? No clue at all." Maisie shook her head. "I don't know why, but I'm actually quite shocked."

"Let's wait and see," Brent said wisely. "And if everything pans out, you won't be the only one who gets a surprise tonight."

CHAPTER 19

Aboard *The Kreltonian Skull* - Andromeda Class Battle Cruiser

Official Status: Insurance Claim Filed.

Ship's Log: Earth Orbit.

Zeb made a rough mental calculation and figured that if he stayed locked in the pitch-black, ice-cold storage bay, he had only 37.549 seconds before he was in serious trouble. He thought about safeguarding his neural net by switching his body to sleep mode and rerouting all power to his head. The electrical activity would keep his neural net warm, but that would only buy him an hour or two at best, and after that, his organic components would be irreparably damaged. It seemed likely that only Admiral Norph had access to the bay, and the Andelian clearly had no intention of releasing him. *Rescue within my survivable timeframe is highly improbable*, he decided. *If I stay here, I will certainly freeze to death*.

There was no doubt in his mind; escape was the only option.

Switching his vision to enhanced infrared, he studied the huge door that sealed the only exit. There was no way to operate the door from within, and its hinges were on the outside. The locking mechanism was concealed within the door itself, but the inner face of the door was made from a seamless sheet of reinforced alloy. Zeb was stronger than his Andelian crewmates, but he couldn't punch a hole in the metal, and any attempt to do so would only result in critical damage. "Think!" he murmured. "What would Dad do?"

The cold was starting to pinch at Zeb's sensors, but the mental image of Dex gave him a little courage, and he set his mind to explore a new path. Dex was an engineer, a problem-solver. Given a technical challenge, Dex would tackle it from a number of different angles, looking for a way in. *Every lock needs a key*, Zeb thought. *How did Norph unlock the door?* Yes. He'd placed his hand on a touch panel on the wall. Zeb sidestepped and examined the wall. He was picking up a faint heat signature from within: a cluster of electronic modules attached to a power supply. That had to be it. Activating each of his enhanced vision modes in turn, he detected a series of stress patterns in the alloy wall panel. And there, running along the panel's edges, were the bolts that held it in place, their heads concealed beneath a thin plastic trim. *No problem.*

Working as quickly as his cold joints would allow, Zeb ripped the plastic strip from the panel's perimeter, revealing the heads of a row of gleaming bolts. He looked at the bolts closely. Each head bore a Torx slot, a star-shaped indentation, and Zeb knew what to do. He pulled the tip from the index finger of his left hand and held it up before his eyes. A slim, metal extension protruded from the joint, and he turned it around. "No, that's a Phillips number two," he muttered, replacing his fingertip. He repeated the process with his forefinger, and this time, he was in luck. The metal tool beneath his fingertip fitted into the slot perfectly, and when he twisted his hand, the bolt turned smoothly. *Power mode*, Zeb thought, and with a whirring whine, his wrist began to rotate, spinning faster and faster, his left hand a blur. A second later, the bolt fell to the floor. Checking how much time he had left, Zeb set to work on the other bolts, selecting one corner of the panel and working along the adjoining sides, removing each bolt in turn.

When the two sides were free, Zeb replaced the tip on his forefinger. Ideally, he would've liked to remove the bolts from all four sides and lift the whole panel out, but there was no time. Around the corner that he'd freed, the crevice along the panel's edge was wide enough to admit his fingers, and he jammed them into the gap, gripping the panel's edge tight and wrenching it away from the wall with all his strength.

The panel budged but only a fraction of an inch. It wasn't enough. "Come on!" Zeb yelled, and with a fresh surge of determination, his auxiliary motors stepped up to full power. The panel was thicker than he'd first supposed, and it resisted his attempt to yank it from the wall. Its edges bit into Zeb's frozen fingertips, but he scarcely felt the pain. Determination fueled his fight, and he clenched his jaw, his neck corded as he strained every synthetic sinew in his body. The panel groaned, emitting a low moan of despair, then suddenly, with the juddering screech of tortured metal, the alloy sheet creased across its center and crumpled beneath his grip.

"Yes!" Zeb roared, his voice hoarse, then he followed through, ripping the panel from the wall. Triumphantly, he threw it aside, but instead of the modules he sought, all he could see was a thick layer of white insulation. He sank his fingers into the soft insulating foam, tearing at it frantically, but his joints were paying the price for his earlier exertions, and his movements were becoming slower, clumsier. Worse, the connections in his neural net were breaking down, his thoughts decaying, growing fuzzy. He ground his teeth together, willing his mind to concentrate. *Find the control module. Find the...control...module.* He swayed as he worked, his limbs weary, but he was almost there. The cluster of modules emerged from the foam, each oblong of pristine plastic glowing bright in his enhanced field of vision. All he had to do was select the right one and then trigger the door lock. But which plastic block was the control module? He blinked, a layer of ice crystals crinkling his thin eyelids. *Which one is it? How do I choose?* Just a moment ago, he'd known exactly what he was looking for, but now the knowledge was slipping away. He grabbed at the nearest module, yanking it roughly from its slot, but nothing happened, and a knot of panic formed in his mind. He had no idea what to do. His neural net was shutting...shutting down. He couldn't...couldn't...

Zeb's shoulders slumped. His head hung low, his chin resting on his chest. He'd failed. *I'm sorry, Dad*, he thought. *I let you down*. And then he knew no more.

***

A dull thud reverberated through the bay, and with a mighty hiss, the door swung wide. The bay flooded with light, and through the clouds of swirling mist that cascaded out through the open door, a figure stepped, a heavy-duty power drill held at shoulder height.

Dex dropped the remains of the door's control panel to the ground and rushed inside, crying, "Zeb! What happened? I picked up your beacon but..." Dex didn't finish his sentence. Instead, he staggered to a standstill, his words left hanging in the icy air. There was no point in saying anything further. No point in hurrying. He was too late.

Slowly, he moved closer to Zeb, taking in the layer of ice that coated the cybonic lifeform's features, the devastated wall panel, the crumbling plastic foam that lay scattered over the freezing floor. He laid his hand on Zeb's shoulder, but of course, there was no response. "Who did this to you?" he whispered. "Why?"

He tore his eyes from Zeb's frozen face and looked

around, a dark horror hollowing him out from head to toe. "Norph!" he growled. "This time you've gone too far!" He hooked his hands firmly beneath Zeb's armpits and pulled him close, dragging him toward the door. "Come on, son," he murmured, sniffing back a tear. "Let's get you fixed up. We'll soon have you good as new. Don't you worry."

Dex lumbered out into the corridor, feeling the warmth flood back into his bones. Some part of his mind told him that Zeb was a heavy burden, but Dex didn't feel the weight, didn't care. He felt only the fire burning in his belly. He'd pay Norph back for this. There were no two ways about it. He'd beat the evil bastard, even if it was the last damned thing he ever did.

CHAPTER 20

UN Space Dock 7 - Earth Orbit

Surrana slunk along pier twelve, her outline mingling with the shadows, her footsteps soundless. There was a small element of risk in her outing, but it was vital that she scouted the length of the pier before the appointed hour of Rawlgeeb's arrival; preparation was everything, and Surrana was more prepared than most. She had taken certain steps to ensure success, but for her peace of mind, she needed to make one last check that nothing in her arrangements had gone awry.

She was not concerned at leaving the hostage unattended for a minute or two. According to the Guild's rules, the female was secure: bound and gagged but in no immediate danger. She was safe in bay three, exactly as arranged, and the handover would be carried out according to all of the Guild's strict conventions. But what happened after the hostage had been exchanged…well, that was another matter entirely. At such times, the Guild allowed each member to give free reign to their creativity. After all, it was in the interests of the Guild if each of its members maintained a certain reputation.

Surrana smiled to herself, whispering the Guild's mantra under her breath, "Death comes on swift wings to the unwary." Overhead, a security drone whirred past on its routine patrol, and she tilted her head, following its path from the sound of its distant engines. She sniffed the air, but all was well. The drone smelled like Earth tech, so it almost certainly belonged to the UN and was, therefore, no threat whatsoever. She had taken care of the UN's security measures earlier in the day, subtly altering the programming of every camera and every drone. Her night's work would go undetected.

She squatted on her haunches, slipping her hand behind a broad pipe. The smooth alloy of the pipe was cold to the touch, filled as it was with highly volatile liquefied fuel, and her fingers soon found the device she'd planted there. The bomb responded to her touch with a soft beep, letting her know that it was armed. Surrana stood slowly, being careful not to disturb the device. *One down*, she thought, *fifteen more to check*.

She straightened, glancing over her shoulder, then she moved swiftly along the pier to the place where the next device was hidden. Blowing up a huge chunk of the space dock hadn't been Surrana's first choice, but certain stipulations had been made. Her employer had insisted that there must be no evidence left behind, and no chance of recovering even the tiniest clue from the scene. In addition, the whole affair must be made to look like an act of terrorism, the blame to be placed firmly on the human resistance movement. Surrana had already prepared the files that would incriminate the humans, and all that remained was to circulate the material to the media networks on Earth and the Gloabon High Command.

Nevertheless, there was a downside to this modus operandi that troubled Surrana even as she worked. There would be no trace of her endeavors, no lasting impression of her style. She prided herself on bringing a certain flourish to her work. The elegant strike from her needle-sharp knife was her signature, and to obliterate that simple elegance with a fiery blast did not sit well with her. She frowned. Covert work paid handsomely, but where was the flair, the finesse, the sense of a job well done? *If I'd wanted simply to destroy lives, I would've become a politician*, she thought. But her work was about something more than that. It was a craft, a unique set of skills. She let a silent sigh whisper from her lips. Truth be told, she was getting a little tired of working for this particular employer. The nature of this latest task betrayed a greedy streak of ambition that seemed un-Gloabon. Such a ruthless thirst for success was more human in nature, and the thought sent a shudder down Surrana's spine. *When this job is done, so am I*, she decided. *No more dirty work for the Gloabon Government. Rawlgeeb will be my last victim.*

CHAPTER 21

UN Space Dock 7 - Earth Orbit

In the shipping container's gloom, Brent leaned closer to the metal crate that supported Vince's laptop. He peered at the shaky image on the screen, but after a few seconds, he shook his head. "Vince, I can't make out a damned thing from the drone. Wouldn't the CCTV be better?"

"I tried the security cameras, but they weren't much help," Vince replied. "My guess is that the assassin got to the CCTV before we did. They're broadcasting images all right, but they've been reprogrammed to show all the wrong places. There are massive blind spots around the area we need, and the only way we can see inside pier twelve is to use the drone. Sorry, but that's the best we can manage right now."

"I guess it'll have to do. But can't you hold the damned thing steady?"

Vince's fingers darted over the laptop's keys. "I'm working on it, but I'm not used to Gloabon drones, and since Rawlgeeb messed with the fuel cells, it's not flying as smooth as it should."

Squatting down beside Vince, Rawlgeeb sighed. "I had no choice. We couldn't afford to arouse the assassin's suspicions, and he would've identified the drone as Gloabon immediately. If you thought my sense of smell was acute, you should witness an assassin's abilities. Their senses are honed to an incredible degree."

"Keep your voice down," Brent murmured. "That kind of talk gives the doc a severe case of the heebie-jeebies, and I need him sharp."

Huddled in the corner, intent on fretting over his machinery, Doctor Cooper raised his head. "Did you mention my name?"

Brent gave him a friendly wave. "Nothing to worry about, Doc. Hey, did you get a trace on our alien friend?"

"Not on the actual, er, the actual…oh my God, what am I doing here?"

"Relax, Doc," Brent said, keeping his voice level. "Just tell me what you *have* found."

Cooper nodded. "All right, but it's bad news. The whole pier is wired with explosives. The devices are small, but their signatures match a type of demolition charge used by the Gloabon military."

Brent whistled. "How are they triggered?"

"Remotely by encrypted radio signal," Cooper replied. "That's standard anyway. For all I know, they may have been modified by the…by the…oh dear God."

"Just say *the target*," Vince suggested. "Keep it professional, Doc. You're doing fine."

"Thank you," Cooper said. "I'll get back to work. If I can analyze the devices, I should be able to isolate the trigger frequency, then maybe I could jam it."

"And how would you do that?" Brent asked.

Cooper blinked. "Easy really. The information will be keyed to the serial numbers of the devices. I can locate the nearest one, I just need somebody to go and bring it back so that I can examine it."

"Oh." Brent scratched his jaw. "I wonder how Maisie's getting on. We're going to need the UN to come through when the heat gets turned up. Maybe I should go check on her."

"Come on, Brent, you can't wriggle out of this," Vince

chided. "We're busy with the drones, and yes I *do* need Rawlgeeb's help because he's the only one who can identify the target. The doc has got his hands full with setting up all that equipment, and since Maisie is doing her best to call in the cavalry, that leaves you. We need to grab one of those devices, so you *have* to do it."

"I know that," Brent said defensively. "I was just thinking that maybe there was another way around the problem. You know, if we take out the target, the bombs won't go off."

"Too risky," Rawlgeeb stated. "There are far too many unknowns, and if we make just one tiny mistake or one false move, the whole place could blow up and take us along with it. No. We have to neutralize the devices."

"All right, goddammit." Brent strode toward the door. "I'm going. Just do me a favor, if anything happens to me, look after Algernon. But don't spoil him. He gets a treat on Sundays–the special food. Just a pinch." He let himself out without waiting for a reply, closing the door carefully behind him.

Outside, Maisie was leaning against a wall, speaking softly into her handset. In the soft shadows cast by the space dock's dim lighting, the delicate curves of her cheekbones were thrown into sharp relief, and her long hair framed her face to perfection, emphasizing the dark beauty of her glittering eyes. For a second, Brent drank in the sight of her. She might be the last good thing he ever saw, the last person he ever spoke to. He could take her by the hand, whisper something sweet in her ear, perhaps allowing, just for a moment, his lips to brush against her soft cheek.

But as Brent watched, Maisie lowered the handset and let out a groan of exasperation. "Bastards!" she hissed.

"No joy?" Brent asked, and she looked up with a start.

"Brent. I didn't see you there." She hesitated. "I've tried explaining to the UN's security people, but no one is taking me seriously. They keep putting me on hold or promising to forward my message in the morning. I suppose I should've known it would be like this. They're nothing more than a bunch of spineless bureaucrats. Pathetic!"

"Anyone left on your list?"

Maisie sighed. "A few. I was going to call my boss. It probably won't do any good. I mean, it's not like he's got anything to do with security, but he *might* pull a few strings, that's if he'll even listen to me in the first place."

Brent took a few steps closer to her. "Maisie, this is just a suggestion, but before you launch into the serious stuff, maybe suggest you might meet up with the guy for a few drinks one day. Something like that. You catch more bees with honey."

"What? Are you seriously suggesting I flirt with him? He's a married man, for God's sake."

"So much the better."

Maisie glared at him. "No! I've spent my whole life fighting against that kind of thing. I refuse to use my looks to gain advantage. Men can talk to me as equals, or they can get the hell out of my way, but I will not pander to some outdated stereotype of women as helpless damsels in need of nothing more than a strong man."

"Preach it, sister," Brent drawled. "Unfortunately for your principles, we're up against a ruthless assassin with superhuman powers, the pier is rigged to blow like the biggest fourth of July you ever saw, and the only folks we have in our corner are a ham-fisted high school dropout, an over-anxious scientist, and an alien who, frankly, sails a little too

167

close to the coast of crazy town on the good ship *USS Unhinged*. On top of all that, I'm about to risk certain death by hopping along to pier twelve to snatch a powerful explosive device from under the nose of the previously mentioned assassin. So pardon me if I ask you to bat your beautiful lashes for five seconds and spoon-feed a middle-aged man a sweet cup of sycophantic shinola. Seriously, forgive me for bruising your sensitivities and nudging you sharply in the seat of your deeply held beliefs. It won't happen again. Ever."

"You're such an asshole," Maisie said. "Why can't you just ask nicely for once? Why do you have to be so melodramatic?"

Brent considered this for a moment. "That would be purely for reasons of style. I'll take it over substance any day of the week."

Maisie tutted. "All right, I'll turn on the charm. It'll take me years to regain my reputation, but anything that stops you spouting nonsense has to be worth a try." She raised her handset with one hand while waving Brent away with the other. "Well, go on then. Go and be a hero. I can't bear to have you standing around to eavesdrop while I humiliate myself, so get lost."

Brent raised his chin. "You think I'm a hero? Cool." He flashed Maisie a smile then strolled away, a spring in his step. But as he neared pier twelve, he slowed his pace, pulling out his handset and calling Vince as quietly as he could: "Any sign of the target?"

"Yes," Vince answered, his voice hoarse with excitement. "We picked her up with the drone. She's exactly where she said she'd be. Bay three. It's down near the far end of pier twelve."

"I don't mean the victim," Brent replied. "I'm talking

about the assassin. Have you picked him out, only I'm getting close to the pier, and I'd kind of like to know if I'm about to run into the dude."

There was a hiss on his handset. "I *am* talking about the assassin, Brent. She's female. Rawlgeeb is certain she's the one."

A lead weight sank in Brent's stomach. *Another woman with an attitude*, he thought. *That's all I need*. An image of Maisie came to his mind, but he tried to push it away. He needed to clear his mind, to focus on the task at hand. "Talk to me, Vince. Is she staying put down there? Is it okay for me to go onto the pier?"

A pause. "Yes. Rawlgeeb thinks she's sticking to an ancient custom. She'll wait until the handover before she makes a move. After that, it could go either way."

"All right. Just point me to the nearest device."

"The doc says he's pinging the coordinates through to your handset," Vince replied. "Tell me when you get close."

"Will do. Hang on." Brent flicked his handset to map mode and located the flashing beacon Cooper had sent. Thankfully, it was placed at the entrance to pier twelve, and it took him only a moment to reach it. "I'm here," he murmured into his handset. "I'm standing next to a big metal tank. Might be fuel inside–I can't tell. Where's the device?"

"Cooper says they're small and round," Vince replied. "That one is quite high, about seven feet off the ground. It might be hidden behind something."

"Gee, do you think?" Brent peered upward, but above him, the tall metal tank was lost in shadow. He could just make out a tangle of twisted cables and metal pipes, but there was nothing that looked out of place, and no sign of anything that could be an explosive device. He reached up, his fingers scraping through layers of accumulated dust and grease. If he could just stretch a little farther, he might have more luck.

"Don't move!"

The softly spoken words shot through Brent like a scalpel slicing into a fresh cadaver. He froze. Rawlgeeb had been right: the assassin was highly skilled. He hadn't heard anyone approach.

"Lower your hands then turn around. Real slow."

Brent frowned. Vince had been sure the assassin was female, but this voice, although wheezy and breathless, was definitely male. Slowly, he brought his hands to shoulder height and turned. "Thank fuck for that!"

The security guard was stocky and armed with a handgun, but he was past middle-age and certainly no assassin. If Brent had to guess, he'd bet on the guy being an ex-cop, the nightwatchman's job a way to bump up his pension and keep him from sitting on his ass watching quiz shows on TV.

"Watch your lip, buddy," the guard growled, shining his flashlight in Brent's eyes. "You're in enough trouble already."

"Sorry about that," Brent said. "Listen, could you just shine your light up there for me? There's something I need to see."

The guard stared, unblinking. "What the fuck?"

"I'm serious. It's important."

"Forget it, pal." The guard waggled his pistol. "Start talking. What's your name? And what the fuck do you think you're doing on my dock?"

"Name's Bolster. I'm an investigator. AGI." Brent toyed with the idea of giving the guard the full picture, but his instincts told him otherwise. The guy looked like the slow and steady type, and this was no time for procedure. Thinking quickly, he said, "We had a report of someone trying to stowaway on a ship. I think they hid some fake documents up here, so, seriously, it would be great if you could help me out with that light."

The guard pursed his lips. "You got some ID?"

"All right, if that's the way you want it. It's in my wallet." Brent reached for his pocket, keeping his movements smooth and deliberate, all the while maintaining eye contact with the guard. "I'm a platinum member, actually." Brent produced his wallet, opening it to show his ID.

The guard looked unimpressed. Then his mouth hung open and his eyes glazed over.

"Hey, are you all–" Brent started to ask, but before he could complete his sentence, the guard's knees gave way, and he crumpled to the floor, landing face down with a muffled thud, his pistol and flashlight skittering across the ground, the flashlight's beam extinguished.

"Shit!" Brent pressed himself back against the metal tank, looking wildly from side to side. There was no one in sight, but that didn't mean a thing. The guard must've been killed by a sniper. There was no obvious bullet wound, but with a Gloabon assassin on the loose, there were any number of possibilities; anything from a primitive poison dart to a blast from a sophisticated ray gun. With shaking hands, Brent pocketed his wallet and raised his handset, whispering, "Vince, I'm under fire. Where is she?"

"Damn!" Vince replied. "We saw her lift a weapon, but she's staying put in bay three. What happened? Did she see you?"

"No. There was a guard. He snuck up on me, shone a light. I guess that's what gave him away."

There was a pause before Vince spoke again. "Listen, Brent. We're pretty sure she hasn't seen you. The guard was unlucky. He just got in the way, but I don't think he spooked her. She's standing very still like she's waiting. We could distract her, then you can make a run for it."

Brent ground his teeth together "Sounds good, and believe me, I'd love to get out of here, but I don't have the device. I didn't have time to find it."

"Shit!"

"My thoughts exactly," Brent muttered. "I think it's just above me, but I can't see it. What's the plan for creating a distraction?"

"We'll buzz her with the drone."

Brent swallowed hard, then he reached out his foot and nudged the guard's flashlight a little nearer; there was a still a chance it might work. "All right. Go for it. Tell me when she's looking the other way."

"Hold on. The drone's getting closer. Closer. Now! She's on the move. Shit! She's shooting at the drone!"

In one motion, Brent stowed his handset in his pocket and scooped up the flashlight, sliding the switch back and forth. At first, it didn't work, but he hammered the flashlight's body against his hand and was rewarded with a beam of light. He directed it against the tank, and there it was: the device nestled among the wires, its dark outline clear to see. Brent switched the flashlight off while grabbing the device with his other hand. Feeling the bomb come away in his hand, he turned and fled, running faster than he'd ever run before. He changed direction, heading into the shadows, and in seconds, he was back at the shipping container. As he approached, the door swung open, Maisie beckoning him inside, and he flew through the door, almost barreling into Rawlgeeb. "Sweet Jesus!" he breathed. "That was close. Did she see me? Is she on to us?"

But Vince shook his head sadly. "We have no idea. She took out the drone."

"Is there another drone you can use?" Maisie asked.

"Yes," Rawlgeeb replied. "We brought two of them down into the yard, but you'll have to wait until I've altered the settings on the fuel cells."

"No can do," Maisie said. "We'll have to use the drone as it is. We have to press ahead with the plan now."

"You got through to your boss?" Brent asked. "He'll do what we want?"

Maisie nodded, her expression pinched, her lips tight. "We have everything we need, but the clock is ticking. In fifteen minutes, a team from the UN Special Forces will arrive, and they won't be subtle. Before they start kicking in doors and hollering the place down, we'll need Breamell secure and the target incapacitated."

"Maisie, I said *backup!*" Brent protested. "I wanted a few goons to charge in and secure the area in case things go belly up, not a full-scale invasion."

"I'm sorry," Maisie said primly, "but I wasn't getting anywhere, so I took a leaf out of your book and laid it on a bit thick."

Brent frowned at Maisie, but he couldn't stay angry at her when she met his gaze with those soft brown eyes. "All right, you heard the lady. Time to rock and roll. Vince, get that bird in the air. Doc, get to work on this." He handed the explosive device to Doctor Cooper who took it so gingerly it almost slipped between his fingers. "Easy there, Doc. Rawlgeeb, you're up. Are you ready?"

Rawlgeeb hesitated. "I'm worried. What I'm wearing…it's a dead giveaway. The assassin will guess what we're up to."

Vince stood, peeling off his trench coat. "Here, take this."

"Oh, I couldn't," Rawlgeeb protested. "It's brand new."

"Take it." Vince held out the coat, and Rawlgeeb took it gratefully, slipping it on and fastening the belt.

"There's just one thing missing." Maisie stepped close to Rawlgeeb, turning up the coat's collar then standing back to admire her handiwork. "Now, you're ready."

"Yes," Rawlgeeb said. "Yes, I believe I am."

CHAPTER 22

UN Space Dock 7 - Earth Orbit

Surrana had been lounging against the wall, but now, she stood straight, her slim rifle pressed against her shoulder. Someone was coming, and after recent events, her senses were on high alert. There was no way that security guard should've come bumbling onto the pier; he shouldn't have been anywhere near. She'd checked the rosters and patrol routes, and she'd chosen the handover location and the time very carefully. *What brought him over here?* she asked herself. *Did I leave a trail? Did I give myself away?* She shook her head. She didn't make careless mistakes; not ever. She'd covered her tracks, taking pains over every detail. The guard's unexpected appearance had been one of those random errors that sometimes occurred. But she'd taken care of him, and later, the explosion would dispose of his body. All her plans would come to fruition; there could be no other way.

Even so, a nagging doubt crept into her mind: *What about the drone?* She'd spent a long time reprogramming the automated security protocols, so why had that damned drone come so close to her? Another random error? A glitch in its programming? What else could it be?

Heavy footsteps rang out on the pier's metal walkway, and Surrana stilled her mind. The incident with the drone was of no consequence. Its cameras could not have detected her. As far as the space dock's monitoring systems were concerned, she was invisible. She stood at the center of an electronic blind spot. Her work had been faultless. Only a Gloabon drone could've detected her, and that was unthinkable; she'd have smelled its fuel cells instantly.

The footsteps were closer now, the sound reverberating in the stillness. *His steps are heavy with dread*, she told herself.

Soon, his fear will be no more. Rawlgeeb must've known the price he'd have to pay. The bargain was as old as history: a life for a life. In a way, the undeniable symmetry of the deal had a certain inevitable elegance.

In front of Surrana, Breamell sat very still on an upturned crate. The hostage was expertly bound and gagged, but even so, the young female's reserve had impressed her. Most of Surrana's captives moaned and wept bitter tears of anguish, but Breamell, after a brief struggle, had maintained a stony silence, her back straight, her shoulders square. Surrana was almost tempted to let her live. Almost.

"I believe your friend will be with us shortly," Surrana murmured. "When I'm satisfied that he has come prepared to give himself over to me, I shall untie you, allowing you a brief moment of freedom. Enjoy it while you can–it won't last."

It was vaguely irritating that the girl didn't sob at the cruelty of her last remark, but Surrana let it go. A tall figure had appeared at the bay's entrance: Rawlgeeb, his form little more than a silhouette, his outline picked out by the low glimmer of the pier's lights. He turned to face her, his eyes seeking her out, and as he moved, the tails of his long coat swirled out around his legs.

"I am here as you requested," he called out, his voice edged with steel. "Let Breamell go, and I *might* let you live."

Surrana fought down the bark of laughter that threatened to bellow from her throat. She opened her mouth to reply, but in that moment, she detected a faint whirring sound from above her. She sniffed the air. "You have a Gloabon drone. So what? Did you expect me to surrender?" Despite herself, she laughed. "Rawlgeeb, I do not care whether we are observed. My mission is sanctioned at the highest level."

Rawlgeeb moved toward her, striding purposefully into the bay. "The High Command? Nonsense!"

"Your faith in them is touching," Surrana said. "I pity you, really I do. They used you, Rawlgeeb, or at least, they tried to. But you didn't play ball, and now you have to pay the price." She leveled her weapon at his head. "That's far enough."

Rawlgeeb stopped walking. "What you say is simply not true. I have obeyed my orders faithfully. I'm already on the trail of the missing people, and I have obtained a vast amount of data. You must explain why I've been targeted. You owe me that much. We both know I'll take the knowledge to my grave."

"Perhaps." Surrana hesitated. The drone was closer now. What was it doing? And who had sent it? Was Tsumper trying to double-cross her? She blinked, focusing on her target. She could not kill Rawlgeeb until the exchange had been made; her status as a Guild member was at stake. But this was taking longer than she'd planned. It was time to wrap it up. "Rawlgeeb, there are forces at work within the High Command that you will never understand. You think Commander Tsumper is on your side, but it was she who tasked me with Breamell's capture."

"What? She sent you to…to kill me?"

"No," Surrana replied. "She merely wanted pressure brought to bear on you. But I have instructions from another source: a higher authority. Let us just say that the orders came from further up the food chain—from one level above poor old Tsumper to be precise."

Rawlgeeb leaned back as though she'd punched him on the chin, but for the sake of Breamell, he recovered his equilibrium quickly. "All right. I submit myself freely. By the terms of our ancient customs, I ask you to release your hostage."

Surrana smirked. "Very good. Start walking but keep your hands where I can see them." Rawlgeeb did as he was told, and Surrana moved to Breamell's side. "Run to your friend, my dear. These are the last moments of his life. They are precious. Do not disappoint him by forcing my hand, or even those fleeting seconds will be lost. Do you understand?" The girl nodded, and Surrana freed her, pulling her bindings away with a deft flick of her wrist. "Go," she said.

Breamell sprang up from her seat and ran to Rawlgeeb, barreling into him, hugging him fiercely as he wrapped his arms around her. "Rawlgeeb, I'm so sorry. She caught me unawares. There was nothing I could do." She hesitated. "What…what's this under your coat?"

"Shush," Rawlgeeb whispered. "Just hold on tight to me. Whatever happens next, just hold on tight."

"That's enough," Surrana snapped. "Breamell, back away from him, or I'll kill you both where you stand."

Surrana brandished her rifle, but Rawlgeeb did not comply. He stared up into the sky, and for a split second, Surrana was sure that his nerve had finally given out; he was ready to accept his fate. She'd seen many people face their deaths, and more than a few had cried out to the heavens, hoping in their last moments for some miracle to save them. But Rawlgeeb did not let out the pleading wail she'd expected. He simply said one word: "Now!"

CHAPTER 23

UN Space Dock 7 - Earth Orbit

Brent eased his way carefully through the maintenance shaft, grasping at each handhold set into the floor and pulling himself along. The pouch strapped to his chest wasn't helping any, but there was no way around that. He looked ahead, searching the blank metal walls for some sign that his journey was nearly at an end, but there was nothing.

He crawled on, dragging his body forward, hand over hand. The shaft that ran around the perimeter of the vast, orbiting space dock was usually reserved for the runner-bots that delivered spare parts, and its bare metal walls were stark and forbidding, pressing in on him from every side. But what was that up ahead? Yes. A hatch. His arms moved faster, and soon, the hatch was right in front of him. He wiped grime from its label. "Bay three," he read. "Finally." Gripping its handle, he slid the hatch open, easing it gently along its recessed track. When the gap was wide enough to admit his shoulders, he leaned forward, peering down into the vast bay.

A long way below, he could just make out the shapes of Rawlgeeb and his antagonist. Between them, the third shape must be Breamell. It looked as though she was still tied to a chair, though he couldn't be sure. Fortunately, he didn't have to rely on his own eyesight; Vince was monitoring the situation closely via the reserve drone. The flying machine was out of Brent's eye line, but he could hear its motors churning the air somewhere below him, and he hoped the sound would prevent the assassin from hearing him when he climbed out from the shaft. *So far, so good*, Brent told himself. He put his handset to his ear. "Vince, I'm almost in position," he whispered. "Ping me the coordinates."

"Done," Vince murmured. "By the way, we think we've jammed the bombs."

"You *think?*"

"Yeah. We can't be one hundred percent sure. It's not like we can test it. What was that, Doc?" A pause. "The Doc says, ninety-nine point nine percent certain. I guess that'll have to be near enough."

"I'll take his word for it," Brent replied. "Keep an eye on Rawlgeeb. I have to move." He pulled up the map on his handset then looked out across the maze of interconnected girders and pipes below, orienting himself with his screen. "Oh shit!" According to the coordinates Vince had just sent him, his destination lay at the far end of the bay, and as far as he could see, the only way to reach it was via a narrow, suspended footbridge, its thin metal struts looking no more substantial than toothpicks. He glanced down to the bay floor, estimating how far he'd fall if he slipped. *Too god-damned far*, he decided. *Way, way too goddamned far*. He swallowed hard, clenching his jaw and forcing down the wave of fear swelling in his chest. He *had* to take the bridge; there was no other route. "Why do they always put important things in places that are so goddamned hard to get to?"

He squeezed out through the hatch, lowering his feet onto the bridge's first slender strut. The footbridge bobbed beneath his weight, and he clung to the flimsy handrail for dear life, a swirl of nausea churning in the pit of his stomach. "Come on, Bolster," he scolded himself from between clenched teeth. "Just put one foot after another."

Brent squared his shoulders and started forward, staring straight ahead at the small metal platform that was his goal. The next few seconds sapped every ounce of energy from his body. He could feel his life force draining away into the shadowy depths below. But he kept moving until he could clamber onto the platform, his leg muscles quivering, his breath coming in short, tight gasps.

Leaning heavily against the wall, Brent took out his handset. "Vince, I made it," he began, his words punctuated by sharp intakes of breath. "Is this a bad time to tell you about my fear of heights?"

"But, Brent, you don't have a problem with high places."

"I do now," Brent shot back. "My God! I'll never be the same again."

"Take it easy, Boss," Vince replied. "Get your gear ready and stand by for the signal."

"Sure." Brent wiped the sweat from his brow. "And don't call me *Boss*. You're fired, remember?"

"And he's back on form," Vince said. "Check your gear carefully, Brent. And good luck."

"Amen to that." Brent dropped his handset into his pocket and pulled the breathing apparatus from the pouch on his chest. He fitted the mask over his face and checked the seals, taking a few deep breaths to test its efficiency. The pouch hung from a sturdy harness that fitted tightly over his shoulders and around his chest, with another strap that ran between his legs. *Designed for masochists by a sadist*, Brent decided. But it would do its job, or so he hoped.

Working quickly and regaining his strength all the time, Brent pulled the stout cords from his harness and clipped them onto the anchor points in the wall. He flexed his fingers while studying the control panel in front of him. And in his pocket, his handset began to vibrate.

He grabbed the handset, checking the screen. A code was displayed, and Vince wouldn't have sent it unless it was time to use it. This was the signal he'd been waiting for. *Thank you, Mayor Enderley*, Brent thought as he typed. It had taken only one phone call for the mayor to come through with the goods. In fact, the man's speed and efficiency in providing a top-secret access code had sent a shudder down Brent's spine; the mayor was a powerful ally, but he would make a deadly enemy. *When we've finished here, I still need to clear up this case*, Brent reminded himself. *But we're getting closer—I can taste it.* All they needed was a lucky break, and he had a feeling he was just about to get one.

"Bolster's first law," Brent muttered as he typed in the final digit, "there is *always* a manual override code." And far below him, to the deafening blare of a raucous siren, the great bay doors shot open.

CHAPTER 24

UN Space Dock 7 - Earth Orbit

Rawlgeeb pressed his grav boots hard against the floor, and a split second later, the siren screeched its warning. The assassin wheeled around to stare at the door behind her, and Rawlgeeb seized his chance. "Use this," he yelled to Breamell, opening his coat with one hand while he kept the other wrapped tight around her. He scrabbled for the breathing apparatus strapped to his chest and saw with relief that Breamell was following his example. "Hold on to me," he called out, his voice muffled, but he needn't have worried; Breamell clung to him like an Andelian death limpet, her strong arms almost squeezing the breath from his lungs.

"No!" the assassin screamed, but her cry was whisked away by the whirling rush of escaping air. The artificial gravity had cut out as soon as the door was opened, and the assassin was plucked from the floor as if by invisible fingers, the sheer force of the air currents wrenching the rifle from her grip. The drone, along with the upturned crate Breamell had sat on, hurtled out through the doors and into space, tumbling wildly as they vanished into the inky darkness. But by some feat of gymnastic ability, the assassin turned in midair, twisting her body and diving toward the wall. She grasped a rail and hung on, planting her feet against a pipe and crouching there like a vengeful demon. She fixed Rawlgeeb with her gaze, her dark glare piercing him to the core, and Rawlgeeb knew exactly what she was thinking. Soon, the air in the bay would all be gone, and then, with no force to oppose her and no gravity to hold her back, she would launch herself at them both, killing them in an instant.

Rawlgeeb took a faltering step backward, fighting against the rushing air that still tugged at his coat as if trying to tear it from his body, but there was no point in trying to run. Despite the lack of oxygen, the assassin was calm and composed, readying herself, tensing her muscles. *I've screwed up*, Rawlgeeb realized. *I haven't done enough*. Why hadn't he thought further ahead? Why hadn't he allowed for this eventuality? This was an assassin he was dealing with. An assassin!

Rawlgeeb racked his brains, but there wasn't much he could do. Not now. He looked down at Breamell, and she gazed up at him, looking deep into his eyes. But he saw no despair in her expression, only passion and fire: the desperate will to survive. *I'll save her*, he told himself. *I cannot let her die. I* will *not*.

Squaring his shoulders, Rawlgeeb delved into his coat pocket. There was nothing there except for the handset Vince had given him, but he pulled it out, an idea forming in his mind. The sequence of digits that he needed came easily to his fingertips as he typed, and he knew that if there was one thing in the galaxy he could rely on, it was the predictability with which his people would follow official procedures. He had served the Gloabon bureaucratic machine for his entire life, and now, that ponderous, administrative goliath was about to save his life.

The flow of air was reducing already, but the assassin was apparently able to hold her breath for long periods without concern. No doubt she calculated that she could survive long enough to complete her task. Rawlgeeb looked down at Breamell. "Let go!" he called out. "It'll be all right."

"No!" Breamell shouted back. "Never."

But Rawlgeeb had no time to explain; the rush of escaping air was at an end. The assassin launched herself at her intended victims, and Rawlgeeb prised Breamell's arms from his body. Her grip was tight, but he was stronger, and he gave her a shove, pushing her upward and away across the bay, her body twirling in zero-G. Held in place by his grav boots, Rawlgeeb stood firm when the assassin collided with him, her left arm snaking around his shoulders, her right arm ready to strike, something glinting in her fist. But Rawlgeeb was ready, the handset pressed hard against his breathing mask, the emergency sampling codes already entered. "Sample to zip up!" he shouted. And as the assassin's hand flew toward his throat, a wave of ice washed over him, and the gloomy bay winked out of existence.

CHAPTER 25

UN Space Dock 7 - Earth Orbit

Brent stared down into the bay for several seconds before he made the call. "Vince," he began, but no more words would come to mind.

"Brent! What happened?" Vince asked. "Are they safe? Did it work?"

"Yes and no," Brent replied. "I can't see much from up here, but it looks like Breamell is okay. The assassin has gone, but...so has Rawlgeeb."

"What?"

"Yeah. He sort of grabbed hold of the assassin and took him. I guess he got them zipped back to the space station." Brent hesitated. "And the girl...she's still floating around. She's got a mask on, but if I shut the doors she'll drop like a stone."

"I'll come along and help," Vince said. "We have spare grav boots here, so...oh shit!"

"What's happened?"

Vince sighed. "It's the cavalry—the UN. The doc picked up their signal a minute ago, and he says their shuttle just docked. You'd better get out of there. Stay safe, Brent. Don't go shooting your mouth off and antagonizing a bunch of heavily armed goons."

"What do you mean?" Brent demanded. "I never antagonized anyone in my whole life. Ask your mother–she always speaks so fondly of me when we're in that cheap motel she likes."

"Forget it!" Vince snapped, and he disconnected the call.

"Ah well," Brent muttered, pocketing his handset. "Just

another day at the office." He held onto the platform's hand-rail. Was it just his imagination or was that vibration caused by the the rumble of boots? He grimaced. The booming rhythm of double-time footsteps was one of his least favorite things; in his experience, it generally came just before a whole heap of trouble. *Discretion is the better part of Valerie,* he thought and eyed the narrow footbridge warily. *Let the goons rescue the girl,* he decided. *It'll give them something to boast about in the bar later.* Smiling, Brent stepped onto the bridge. The maintenance shaft was beckoning, and the more distance he could put between himself and the bay, the less explaining he might have to do later. And that was worth every death-defying step on the swaying bridge.

CHAPTER 26

Aboard *The Kreltonian Skull* - Andromeda Class Battle Cruiser

Official Status: Missing - Written Off Against Taxes.

Ship's Log: Earth Orbit.

Chief Engineer Dex wiped the oil from his hands with a rag. "I've done my best," he murmured. "The rest is up to you." He patted Zeb on the chest, but the cybonic science officer lay still on the workbench, his eyes closed. Dex took a breath and picked up the final cable. Once this lead was inserted into the universal interface on the side of Zeb's head, the science officer's neural net should come back online, rebooting from its deep hibernation mode. If it didn't work, Dex might just have to accept that Zeb was gone. *Never*, he told himself. *One way or another, I'm bringing him back.* Checking the plug's orientation carefully, Dex went to make the connection. But something was wrong. "Oops! I've got the dratted thing upside down." Turning the plug around and peering intently at the interface, he slid the plug home, and it engaged with a satisfying click.

"Come on, son," Dex whispered. "You can do it, I know you can."

But there was no response.

Dex sighed, scraping his hand down his face. "Where did I go wrong? Did I miss a step out?" He shook his head. He'd always been a careful man, following every procedure in the minutest detail, and while working on Zeb, he'd taken great pains to restore every joint, every servo, every motor. But recovering an advanced neural net that had been practically shut down for so long? To his knowledge, it had never been done before. No one had even tried.

"I need a break," Dex muttered to the empty room. He'd stretch his legs and fetch himself a hot drink. Then, when he'd had a few minutes to mull the problem over, the answer would come to him. It *had* to. "I'll be right back," he said to Zeb, and with heavy steps, he trudged from the room.

***

Dark. Pain. Zeb's eyes fluttered open, and he stared up at the ceiling. He blinked, turned his head. This was the engineering bay; the place he'd been born. "Hello?"

No reply. No sound. He was alone.

Stiffly, Zeb sat up, a cable tugging at the side of his head. He reached up, his fingertips gingerly probing the edge of his interface, and instinctively knew what it was. "All right. This is good." The cable was bringing a gentle trickle of power to his awakening neural net, but it also provided something else. *I'm online,* Zeb told himself. *I can access the ship's main computer. I can access EVERYTHING!*

The door slid open, but the man entering the bay seemed to be having some sort of seizure. He threw a cup of liquid into the air, waving his arms and letting out a strange yelping sound. Ah. Yes. This was also good. It was very good indeed.

Zeb smiled. "Hey, Dad. I'm back."

CHAPTER 27

Gloabon Space Station *The Gamulon* - Earth Orbit

Rawlgeeb rubbed his eyes, and the room swam into focus. Unfortunately, so did the pair of officials in charge of the sampling reception area. They glowered at Rawlgeeb with undisguised hatred, their faces pale with rage.

"What the flek is the meaning of this?" one of them demanded. "You have violated every rule we have. We processed your request in good faith–the records will back us up. But…but we see now that you have no authorization. I've never heard of such a disgraceful breach of protocol. You're not even in proper uniform!"

Rawlgeeb pursed his lips. At one time, he would've cringed beneath such a verbal onslaught, but not anymore. His time on Earth had certainly not been spent in the high-minded pursuit of knowledge, as prescribed by the greatest Gloabon thinkers of the age, but in all sorts of unexpected ways, it had been the most enlightening experience in his life: practically an educational field trip.

Bolster's first law, Rawlgeeb thought. *Make it up as you go along.* And he stiffened his spine. "You! What is your name?" he demanded. "Quickly now."

The official blinked. "Er, I'm Beetfrump, and I happen to be the senior sampling operative on duty." The Gloabon recovered some of his earlier bluster. "And as such, I must protest about your flagrant misuse of sampling protocols."

"Go ahead," Rawlgeeb said. "But where is the sample that I brought in? You managed to separate us in transit, so I presume she was processed correctly and deposited in a cell as per standing order seven-nine-two stroke three, subsection B, paragraph ninety-five?"

"Yes. Naturally." Beetfrump's eyes went to the workstation in front of him. "Well, she was. But it says here that she's a Gloabon, so I expect my guards will have released her immediately."

Rawlgeeb leaned close to Beetfrump. "Your men are already dead," he said slowly.

Beetfrump quailed beneath the weight of Rawlgeeb's words, but he seemed determined to put on a brave face. "I…I think you must be deranged. I've had enough of this. I must report this incident immediately."

"Good. Get on with it," Rawlgeeb snapped. "Do it this instant. Get hold of Shappham. I want to talk to him right now."

"The Head of Sampling Records? I can't do that," Beetfrump replied. "He'll be asleep."

Rawlgeeb bared his teeth. "Do I look like I give a rat's ass about what he's doing?" Get him out of bed and tell him to meet me in the Liaison Unit. Then you'd better send someone down to the cells with a mop and bucket." He paused to let his words sink in. "There's going to be a lot of blood."

Reluctantly, Beetfrump nodded. "All right," he muttered. "I'll call Shappham. But…but what's going on? Who *are* you?"

"My name is Rawlgeeb, and you'd better remember that, because one day, you're going to want to tell your kids about the day I came up here to set things straight." He turned and marched for the door, slamming his palm against the touch panel.

But the door remained shut.

Rawlgeeb took a breath. "Could you…could you just open this door for me?"

Beetfrump hurried over. "Certainly, Rawlgrab."

"Oh, for flek's sake," Rawlgeeb muttered, and as the door opened, he strode outside and headed for his erstwhile place of work. A few things had become crystal clear to him since his encounter with the assassin. There'd been something that she'd said, back at the space dock, that had given him a valuable clue. It was time to put the pieces together, and for that, he'd need someone on his side within the Gloabon hierarchy. He just hoped he'd made the right choice.

CHAPTER 28

Earth UN Headquarters

Brent paced the length of the cell until he reached the barred door, then he turned around and marched back to the far wall.

Maisie cast an annoyed glance in his direction. "Why don't you try the door? That worked so well the last time we were locked in a cell together."

"Tried it twice already," Brent replied. "It didn't do any good."

"You don't say." Maisie regarded him coolly. "Do all your clients wind up behind bars, or am I just unlucky?"

Brent tilted his hand from side to side. "About fifty-fifty. But the way I look at it, I have a fifty percent success rate, and in this line of work, that ain't too shabby."

"Half of your clients are happy with your services?" Maisie asked. "You surprise me."

"No, half of them wind up dead," Brent replied. "Only the lucky ones end up in the clink." He paused, looking thoughtful. "You know, they shouldn't let those guys post reviews online. The standard of grammar in the convict community is not good. You should see some of the death threats I get—very poorly punctuated."

Maisie shook her head. "I'll skip that delight if you don't mind. When I get out of here, I'm going to try very hard to put this whole episode, and you, a long way behind me."

"Yeah, we really should stop meeting like this," Brent shot back. "Still, I guess I should be grateful you're not wearing a ballgown this time."

"Are you giving out fashion tips now?" Maisie asked. "I'm thinking of putting in a stint in Sing Sing in the fall, what should I wear, old-school stripes or just plain orange?"

Brent bit back his reply, mainly because he couldn't think of a remark that Maisie, in her present mood, wouldn't tear to shreds in an instant. Instead, he turned to Vince and Doctor Cooper. "Are you guys holding up okay?"

Vince shrugged, but Cooper's eyes glittered a little too brightly, his grin unnaturally wide. "I'm fine," Cooper said. "Perfectly fine. As a matter of fact, this place reminds me of the dorms in my old boarding school. The atmosphere of barely restrained violence is the same, but we haven't been thrown into solitary or waterboarded yet, so this beats my first day at St. Cuthbert's hands down."

"Right," Brent replied, stretching the word as much as one syllable would allow. "Doc, don't take this the wrong way, but when we get out of here, you may want to drop by a shrink. A good one. I can give you some names."

"Why would I do that?" Cooper asked, running his hands over his head, his fingertips pressing hard against his scalp. "Do you think…do you think I'm not handling this very well or something?"

Brent hesitated. "No. No reason. It was just a suggestion."

"Let's talk about something else, shall we?" Maisie asked pointedly. "I hope Breamell is okay. The poor kid was upset."

"Upset?" Vince chipped in. "Did you see what she did to those guys up on the docks? Those dudes were Special Forces, but Breamell took out four of them before they managed to get her back down to the floor. One guy was weeping like a baby."

Maisie jutted her chin. "She'd just been through a terrible ordeal. The last thing she needed was some oaf trying to manhandle her. I'd have done the same in her position." She looked thoughtful for a moment. "I wonder if she could give me lessons in self-defense."

"Lord have mercy on us all," Brent moaned.

Doctor Cooper suddenly sat up straight. "Someone's coming."

They all turned to face the door, and a moment later, Breamell appeared, fresh-faced and wearing a brand new jumpsuit. "Hello everyone. Goodness me, look at you all in there. Is it a private party or can anyone join in?"

Brent stepped forward. "You seem…different. Are you okay?"

"Hell yeah," Breamell replied. "The UN boys have been looking after me, and they have this thing called chocolate, and it's real good." She licked her lips. "I wonder if there's any left."

Maisie went to Brent's side. "Breamell, was this chocolate quite dark and bitter? Because if it was, I think the caffeine might–"

"Don't worry about that," Breamell interrupted. "Let's get you out of there. I have so much to tell you."

"We'd love to chat over a cup of…I don't know, milk or something," Brent said, "but our social lives are a little constrained at present on account of us being locked up behind these bars."

Breamell flapped her hands in the air. "Silly boy! All that's taken care of." She leaned her head back and hollered, "Open up cell five!" She giggled. "That was fun. I always wanted to try something like that. It must be great being a guard. It's the big bunches of keys that appeal to me. I'm not sure why."

Brent and Maisie exchanged a look, but before they

could say anything, a harsh buzzing noise blared from above, and the door rattled open.

Breamell chortled. "Let's go! Oh, you have to sign some forms and things before you go, but I've sorted it all out. I think somebody up there likes me."

Cooper stood shakily. "I thought Gloabons didn't believe in any gods."

"I mean up on *The Gamulon*. I'm pretty sure someone's pulling strings for us. It's probably Rawlgeeb." She sighed. "He's incredible, isn't he?"

"I certainly never met anyone like him," Brent agreed as he stepped out through the cell door. "What do you say? Shall we reconvene in my office?"

"Why not?" Maisie said with a resigned shrug. "At least that way Rawlgeeb will know where to find us if he wants to get in touch."

Breamell grinned. "You're so clever, aren't you, Maisie? *Maisie*, what a sweet name. I think we'll be great friends, don't you?"

"Sure," Maisie replied with an uncertain smile. "I guess we'd better go and call a cab."

"There's no need, it's all been arranged," Breamell said. "The UN people are sending a car for us, isn't that awesome?"

"Terrific," Brent said with feeling. "Best news I've heard all day."

Breamell clapped her hands together then led the way along the corridor, the others following wearily in her wake. But Brent cast a backward glance at the empty cell. The way things were shaping up, maybe, just maybe, he'd be better off if he stayed safely behind bars.

CHAPTER 29

Gloabon Space Station *The Gamulon* - Earth Orbit

Rawlgeeb looked up from his workstation to watch Shappham bumbling into the office. For a high-ranking Gloabon, Shappham was heavily built, and some in the office had joked that he'd be better suited to the brigade of security guards than to administrative work. Those same office gossips generally found themselves deployed to the least civilized outposts of the Gloabon Government, where they served out their days renewing the ink pads in rubber stamps or restoring misshapen paper clips to their former glory. Rawlgeeb did not indulge in gossip, and he'd always been particularly careful in his dealings with Shappham. Now, he had to hope that his diligent display of good manners would finally pay off.

Shappham grumbled quietly to himself as he picked his way between the cramped rows of workstations, and when he finally stood over Rawlgeeb, a dangerous level of profound irritation simmered gently behind his watery gaze. "The hell do you mean by this?" Shappham demanded. "Drag me from my bed in the middle of the night, would you? Heard you'd been banished. Good thing too if you ask me."

Rawlgeeb sat back in his chair, and though the gentle voice of self-preservation whispered words of warning in the back of his mind, his newfound courage told self-preservation to shut the hell up and let the grown-ups talk. If everything went as Rawlgeeb expected, his days of apologizing and begging for forgiveness were all but over. "Thank you for coming, Shappham," he began. "I know that this is unorthodox, but I believe that what I have to show you will be of great interest."

"Doubt it," Shappham grunted. "Wasting time. Have you thrown in the cells in a minute."

But Rawlgeeb was not to be deterred. "That would be a missed opportunity, Shappham. I have some valuable information here, and in the right hands, say, someone who knew how to make the best use of it, this information could be *extremely* valuable."

Shappham pushed out his bottom lip, his eyes beetling from side to side. "Talk. You've got ten seconds."

"I have uncovered a conspiracy," Rawlgeeb announced proudly.

"You and every second idiot I talk to," Shappham grumbled. "Eight seconds."

Rawlgeeb took a breath and launched into the speech he'd prepared, his words almost falling over each other in their haste to leave his rapidly flapping lips. "Thousands of humans have been deliberately sampled in error, placed in suspended animation for over a week to create a break in the audit trail, then reclassified under spurious sampling codes and filed as returned, when in fact, they have been permanently abducted. Commander Tsumper tasked me with tracking these missing people, and I subsequently learned that all human investigations into the problem had been disrupted using alien technology which had *not* originated on Gloabon. From this, I infer that an alien race is involved, and so the abducted humans may have been zinged to an unknown location, possibly off-world. This could not have been achieved without the knowledge of someone in the High Command, and this is borne out by that fact that when I began to investigate, an assassin was sent to execute me. I thwarted the attempt, but the assassin revealed that her orders came from one level above Commander Tsumper, in other words, a Gloabon captain. On arriving back here, I cross-referenced the bogus returns with all amendments approved by anyone with the rank of captain or its equivalent civilian status, and that led me to one man."

"Captain Zorello," Shappham put in.

"What?" Rawlgeeb's hand flew to his mouth. "How did you know?"

Shappham grimaced. "I've had my eye on him for a while. And from what you just said, there was only one person who could've altered the sampling records without arousing suspicion. Anyone else accessing the system would've raised flags all over the place, but as the admiral's adjutant, Zorello could do as he pleased." He wrinkled his nose in distaste. "Also, the Gloabon just doesn't smell right. I can always tell."

"So the question is, what do we do about it?" Rawlgeeb licked his lips. "Should we go to the Fleet Admiral?"

"No, the real question is, how do I know you're not part of the plot?" Shappham's piercing gaze reminded Rawlgeeb uncomfortably of the assassin's lethal stare. "You seem to know a lot about it, so maybe Tsumper had good reason to banish you. I can't help but wonder if you just got in over your head. What happened—did you get cold feet? Are you offering up your partners in crime so you can cut a deal?" He grunted. "Well, what do you have to say for yourself?"

Rawlgeeb looked down for a moment, his mind racing. What *was* his role in this conspiracy? He'd been used as a pawn, that much was certain. He'd been the shuttlecock in a deadly game as Zorello played both sides against the middle.

Tsumper's orders had probably arrived by way of Zorello, who could've altered them to suit his own ends. Meanwhile, Zorello had been the official point of contact for both

Fleet Admiral Squernshall and the UN on Earth. Every communication would've passed across his desk, and he'd have been free to interfere as he saw fit. Zorello had hidden in plain sight, plotting his machinations in the comfort of his plush office.

Rawlgeeb had to admit a grudging admiration for Zorello, partly for his sheer bravado, but mainly for his ruthless efficiency. *So how come I've managed to get this far?* Rawlgeeb asked himself. *And why drag me into it in the first place?* And another piece of the puzzle clicked into its allotted home.

Rawlgeeb looked Shappham in the eye. "You sly devil," he murmured. "You're toying with me."

"I have no idea what you mean."

"You can't kid a kidder," Rawlgeeb insisted. "It was you from the start. You knew I'd been fooled into carrying out illegal abductions, and you knew Maisie Richmond worked for the UN. You figured she was high profile enough to cause a stir. And you knew that, as a researcher into Earth-Gloabon relationships, she'd ask difficult questions and pursue the matter through her contacts. That was why you sent Breamell to fetch me."

"I suppose you're not too far off the mark," Shappham admitted with a begrudging smirk. "Go on. See if you can figure it out."

"Almost everyone in Liaison would've processed the return without attending personally, but you knew that I was fussy about these things, and you knew I'd pay special attention if your name was mentioned." Rawlgeeb warmed to his theme, his voice growing louder as he spoke. "You knew I'd go down to the cells and see it through."

"Ambition, even slow and deliberate ambition such as

yours, provides an excellent fulcrum for the right kind of leverage," Shappham explained. "I knew your reputation, and I knew you'd stick your neck out to make sure the woman was returned to Earth."

Rawlgeeb nodded thoughtfully. "I suppose Brent was just a coincidence."

"Who? I've no idea who you're talking about."

"It doesn't matter." Rawlgeeb leaned forward, resting his elbows on his workstation. "But, if you wanted Ms. Richmond returned, why did she still go missing for ten days?"

"Zorello had the whole process automated, and the sequence had already been set in motion. I decided to let it play out." He grinned. "I knew that you would reset her destination codes, but I also knew that you would remember her case and look into it further, especially when she didn't reappear on Earth at the right time. I wanted to engage your awkward streak. I suspected that the breakdown of procedure would gnaw at you until you discovered the root cause." Shappham paused to scratch his chin. "Unfortunately, you got yourself in a brawl and I couldn't get to you without arousing suspicion. I was waiting for you to be released, but Tsumper got to you first. It was very unfortunate."

"This is outrageous," Rawlgeeb spluttered. "You set me up, then you stood back and watched while I got banished."

"In hindsight, it may not have been the best course of action," Shappham admitted. "If it helps, I wasn't planning on leaving you to rot on that dreadful lump of rock. I'd have brought you back here eventually, but in the meantime, I thought there was a chance you'd make some progress on your own. If you look at it in the right way, you'll see it as a mark of my faith in your abilities."

Rawlgeeb stood. "An assassin was sent to kill me! Breamell was kidnapped!"

"I didn't know about any of that, of course. I didn't know what Tsumper was up to, and I had no evidence at all on Captain Zorello. All the credit for uncovering him must go to you."

Despite the blood pounding in his ears and the anger surging through his veins, Rawlgeeb let out a bark of laughter. "It won't though, will it? And please, don't answer that, it wasn't really a question. I know how these things work." He sighed. "You will take the credit, Shappham, and while you get the glory and a huge promotion, I will be reassigned somewhere out of the way so that I don't kick up a fuss. We both know that's what will happen, so please, don't bother blowing smoke up my ass."

Shappham studied Rawlgeeb's expression. "You've changed, Rawlgeeb. There's something different about you. I wonder if I may have misjudged you after all. It strikes me that I could use someone like you on my staff–on my *senior* staff, that is."

"You know what? At one time, I would've bitten your hand off. But now? As far as I'm concerned, you can take this whole sorry business to the Fleet Admiral yourself. You can have all the limelight. I don't care if I don't even get mentioned. I'm done."

"But, we haven't finished the investigation," Shappham protested. "We still don't know where the humans are being sent."

"You'll figure it out soon enough. I've left a full record of the collated data on my workstation. Have at it. There's enough evidence in the audit trail to arrest Zorello, and once you've got him in your clutches, he'll fold soon enough.

They always do."

"Even so–" Shappham began, but Rawlgeeb didn't let him finish.

"Save it," he drawled. "Save it for someone who just might give a rat's ass, but don't under any circumstances, talk to me about it ever again." And with that, Rawlgeeb made for the exit, striding purposefully across the room.

"Come back here!" Shappham thundered. "Where the hell do you think you're going?"

Rawlgeeb paused in the doorway for long enough to say just three words over his shoulder: "I'm going home."

CHAPTER 30

Aboard *The Kreltonian Skull* - Andromeda Class Battle Cruiser

Official Status: Missing - memorial sculpture commissioned.

Ship's Log: Earth Orbit.

Admiral Norph marched onto the bridge, wiping a smear of grease from his lips on the back of his hand. He glared at his officers, almost hoping that one of them would look him in the eye. He hadn't had anyone flogged for hours, and he craved a little excitement to brighten his mood.

He threw himself into his seat, letting out a loud belch, and scowled up at the main screen. But then he realized who he'd just seen standing behind him. He turned his chair around slowly, his eyes bulging. "You!" he bellowed. "What the hell are you doing here?"

Zeb regarded him with a cool eye. "With all due respect, Admiral, I am the ship's science officer, and I am at my station." He tilted his head to one side. "Is there something I can do to assist you?"

Norph bridled. "How did you get out of–" he began, but cut himself short. No one had so much as looked up from their consoles, but Norph knew the other officers were listening to his every word. "Never mind," he growled. "Be about your business."

"Aye, Admiral," Zeb said smartly. "I have an incoming message for you from engineering. Would you like it routed to the XO?"

"I'll take it here, damn you," Norph snapped. "On screen. Quickly!"

"Coming through now, Admiral." Zeb tapped his console and Dex's image appeared on the bridge's main screen.

"Admiral, I'm afraid there's a problem," Dex said, his brow furrowed. "There's been a radiation leak in one of the storage bays, and unless I shut down the engines, the radiation could flood the whole compartment."

"What level?" Norph demanded.

"Level B three," Dex replied. "There's nothing much there besides recycling and waste processing, so we might be able to get by with a running repair, but if we do that, the storage bays will almost certainly be contaminated, and the affected stores will have to be jettisoned. Then we'd have to close the whole level while we carried out a thorough decontamination process, but it shouldn't take more than a couple of months to get the job done. So if you'd rather keep the engines running—"

"No!" Norph bellowed. "Shut down the engines! Immediately! Do it now, you dolt!"

The first officer, Commander Stanch said, "Admiral, if you do that–"

"Silence!" Norph roared. "I want the engines shut down. Contain the radiation at all costs!"

"Aye, Admiral," Dex said. "Engines going offline now. As instructed."

The background hum on the bridge dropped to a murmur.

"Decloaking now," Commander Stanch stated. "Weapons systems offline. Shields inoperative."

"What are you blithering on about?" Norph asked. "Get everything back online."

"If I may interject," Zeb said. "You have just ordered the chief engineer to shut down the engines. As a result, all of our tactical systems will be offline until the engines are re-started. We have maneuvering thrusters only. The system is designed to–"

"I know how the damned thing works!" Norph roared, baring his teeth. "I've been commanding battleships for dec-ades. I'll take no lessons from a jumped up bag of circuit boards." He jumped to his feet, his bolt gun in his hand. "By the gods, I'll do the damned job properly this time!"

"One moment please!" Zeb held up his finger. "Admiral, I have Lord Pelligrew with a priority one message. On screen."

"What?" Norph wheeled around, scowling as an image of a Kreitian's wrinkled face filled the screen. "Pelligrew!"

Lord Pelligrew leaned forward. "Norph, as Commander in Chief of the Andel-Kreit Fleet, I order you to stand down. Surrender yourself immediately."

"Kreitian scum!" Norph hissed. "I'll never surrender to you! Never!"

"Admiral, we have the Kreitian flagship, *The Star of Kreit*, dropping out of warp along with a fleet of eight destroyers," Stanch announced. "Correction…ten, no, twelve destroy-ers."

"Back off, Pelligrew!" Norph yelled. "We'll fight to the death before we give in to you." He turned to Stanch. "Get the engines running. I want weapons and shields online now. Battle stations!"

"As you wish," Pelligrew said. "We have you listed as destroyed anyway, so it really is easier all around this way."

"Admiral, they have locked weapons on us," Stanch stated. "Even if we restart the engines now, we'll be de-stroyed before we can fire a shot."

Norph advanced on Stanch, his bolt gun leveled at the

first officer's chest. "Do as I say, or I'll execute you for cowardice."

"Commander Stanch," Zeb chipped in, "since the Admiral has disobeyed a direct order from his superior, it is your duty as first officer to assume command of the ship. I for one stand ready to assist you."

Stanch stood perfectly still, his back ramrod straight. He did not take his eyes from Norph, but his hand crept to his sidearm. "It's over, Admiral. Stand down. This is your last chance."

Norph raised his arm, aiming his weapon at Stanch's head. "And those were your last words."

The sharp crack of a bolt gun echoed across the bridge. No one moved.

Admiral Norph froze, his expression fixed in a furious snarl, then he fell heavily, landing flat on his back, his weapon clattering across the deck. His eyes stared upward, unseeing, as a pool of dark blood crept from beneath his head and seeped across the deck.

All eyes went to Zeb, to the bolt gun in his hand.

With a deft movement, Zeb returned his sidearm to its holster. "In the pursuance of my duties as an officer, I have taken the action necessary to preserve the lives of almost all the ship's company. However, I am happy to surrender myself into custody pending a full investigation."

Stanch studied him for a moment. "That won't be necessary, Lieutenant Commander. Stay at your post. Comms, hail *The Star of Kreit* and inform Lord Pelligrew of our surrender."

The comms officer, Ensign Chudley said, "Aye, Commander. Transmitting message now." She turned in her seat, her legs crossed demurely. "Commander, *The Star of*

Kreit are confirming receipt of our surrender and ordering us to stand by for their boarding parties."

"Good," Stanch said. "And Ensign, go and change out of that short skirt."

"But Admiral Norph–" Chudley protested.

"Norph is dead," Stanch said. "And from now on, we all dress in the standard issue uniform. Things need to change around here fast. If we're lucky, they might just let us rejoin the Andel-Kreit fleet." He strode across the bridge and faced Zeb. "We owe you a great debt. We've all kowtowed to Norph and his ilk for too long. But when it counted, you had the courage to break free."

"That's right," Lieutenant Turm put in. "You've come such a long way, Zeb. You'll be an example to the fleet–a true hero."

"Thank you," Zeb replied. "But please, don't call me a hero. I did what I had to do. It was just the way I was raised."

CHAPTER 31

Earth

Brent stared at his handset for a full second after the call ended, then he tossed the device onto his desk and stared across his office.

"What's up?" Vince asked, looking up from his laptop. "You look like you've just seen a ghost."

Maisie had moved the visitors' chair so she could sit beside Vince, and she leaned forward to study Brent's expression. "Tell us, Brent. Who called? Was it Rawlgeeb?"

At the mention of Rawlgeeb's name, Breamell, who'd been curled up in the corner, fast asleep on the floor, stirred and sat up, rubbing her eyes with her fists. "What's happened to him? Where is he?"

"It wasn't Rawlgeeb," Brent said quickly. "It was the mayor. He was calling to congratulate me." He caught the full force of Vince's frown and added, "*Us*, he wanted to congratulate all of us."

"But, we didn't really achieve anything," Maisie protested. "We didn't find a single missing person."

"Seems like Rawlgeeb came through," Brent explained. "Under my mentorship and skilled guidance, he managed to put the pieces together, and he went straight to the Gloabon authorities."

"Was it something to do with Commander Tsumper?" Breamell asked. "The assassin mentioned her name."

Brent ran his hands across his brow. "Turns out it was some guy named Zorello. He masterminded the scheme and ran it on his own. He fixed the system so that the wrong people would get snatched, then he packed them off to the sleep pods on the space station for ten days. He kept them on ice to let the trail go cold."

"Is that what happened to us?" Maisie asked.

"Yup. But we got lucky," Brent replied. "Rawlgeeb played it by the book. He corrected the records and made sure we were tagged with the correct destination codes. We got delayed en route, but that's all."

Vince whistled. "Lucky is right. What happened to the others?"

"This Zorello bastard shipped them off to some Andelian nutjob who…" he hesitated. "There's no nice way to say this. He was fixing to eat them, feed them to his people. He wanted to turn the whole planet into a factory farm for the benefit of a breakaway bunch of Andelians, and Zorello was setting it all up. Later on, the Andelians were going to help Zorello overthrow the Gloabon presence on Earth. I guess they figured they'd divide the spoils between them."

"Ugh!" Breamell, wide awake now, shot to her feet. "Disgusting! I've never heard anything like it."

"I suppose, to some species, there's no difference between them eating a human and us eating a cow," Maisie said.

Breamell shook her head. "That's not what I meant. Their plan was a horrible violation of our procedures. A blatant misuse of resources. It makes me feel sick just to think about it."

"Speaking on behalf of the human race," Brent drawled, "I thank you for your concern."

Vince leaned back in his chair, coupling his hands behind his head. "So it's all over. Case closed. It's a damned shame we didn't get there ourselves, but yay for Rawlgeeb." His smile faltered, a flicker of doubt in his eyes. "Gee, I just hope the green guy is all right. The way he took on that assassin–that was something else."

"He was incredible." Breamell sniffed noisily. "I must get back to *The Gamulon*. I need to find him and make sure he's all right. I don't know what I was thinking, but after that chocolate, I just…" She suppressed a sob. "If anything has happened to him, I'll never forgive myself. I must go. Right now. Could you help me to get a shuttle?"

"That won't be necessary," someone said, and a dark figure appeared in the doorway, its face concealed in the hallway's perpetual gloom.

While they'd been talking, they hadn't noticed the door swinging open, but now, they all turned to stare at the new arrival.

"It's all right, Maisie," Vince said, standing tall with his shoulders back. "I'll protect you."

Brent couldn't help but notice the admiration in Maisie's eyes when she looked at Vince, but he had neither the time nor the patience for drama; he stayed exactly where he was, lounging on his chair. "Come in, Rawlgeeb," he called out. "And quit fooling around."

Rawlgeeb stepped inside, grinning. "Come on, you must allow me to make my grand entrance." He adopted an exaggerated American accent and added, "After all, I did haul your sorry asses out of the fire on this job."

Maisie raised an eyebrow and glanced at Brent, her look telling him precisely who she blamed for Rawlgeeb's bizarre new mode of speech. But even Maisie had to smile when Breamell hurled herself at Rawlgeeb, wrapping her arms around him and plastering kisses on his cheek.

"Take it easy, sweet–," Rawlgeeb began, but when he noticed Vince shaking his head vigorously, he changed his mind. "Er, sweet female who I respect as an equal."

"Oh, Rawlgeeb," Breamell murmured softly, laying her head on his chest. "I'm so glad you're safe. I don't know how I can ever repay you."

Rawlgeeb smirked and opened his mouth, but before he could speak, Brent cut in: "So, you did it, Rawlgeeb. Well done. I guess you two will be buzzing off back to your space station, and all's well that ends well." He rubbed his hands together briskly. "This case is done and dusted. Signed, sealed, and delivered. No liability accepted for errors or omissions. Contents may settle in transit. The value of your investment can go down as well as up. Your actual mileage may vary."

"Brent, what on Earth are you rambling on about?" Maisie demanded. "Did something hit you on the head in that space dock? Or did you just go without oxygen for too long?"

Brent waved her objections away. "Now that the case is over, I have to run through the legal terms and conditions. Official investigator stuff. You wouldn't understand." He looked Rawlgeeb in the eye. "Seriously though, what I said about there being no liability and all, that still stands. I mean, we never had a contract or anything. You didn't hire me, and you're certainly not an employee, so no harm, no foul. No loitering. No fishing. No U-turns. Nothing."

"Wait a minute," Vince chipped in. "You got like this once before, back when old Mrs. Harrigan's husband turned up all by himself, but she still paid her bill anyway." His hand flew to his mouth. "Did Mayor Enderley *pay* you? Did he give you the cash, even though Rawlgeeb did all the work?"

Brent tried for an inscrutable expression, but failed miserably; it wasn't easy to appear nonchalant when a room full of people were glaring at him, their hard eyes alight with incredulous anger.

"Brent!" Maisie spluttered. "You took the money and you were going to keep it for yourself! How could you? Of all the low-down, sneaky, dishonest little–"

Her flow of invective was just getting up a decent head of steam when it was drowned out by the hoarse, braying sound that passed for a guffaw from Rawlgeeb. The alien stepped back from Breamell's embrace and bent double, slapping his thighs and hooting like a half-strangled owl.

Breamell patted him on the back. "There, there. It's all been too much for you, Rawlgeeb. You need a rest and a nice bath. I could come with you and rub your back. If you'd like me to, that is."

Rawlgeeb straightened up, wiping his eyes and patting Breamell affectionately on the arm. "Thank you, but I'm all right. I'm just fine. In fact, this is all too perfect. It's ridiculously hilarious, and also, very wonderful at the same time." He chortled but fought to control it. "You see, I had this dream, this crazy idea, but I couldn't see how it could work. And now this! This changes everything."

"I'm not with you," Brent said. "Listen, you did a swell job and everything, and maybe I could send you a few credits to take care of your expenses, like to maybe get yourself a top-class Gloabon head doctor if there is such a thing. And take my advice, I mean a really *top-notch* professional, because the last time I saw anyone laugh like that, they were one short step away from hiding bodies in the freezer, know what I'm saying?"

"No, not really," Rawlgeeb replied. "But the thing is this.

I came down here for two reasons. One, I had to find Breamell."

"Aw!" Breamell nestled against him.

"Two," Rawlgeeb went on, "I wanted to offer you a proposition, Brent. Can't you guess what I'm going to say? You *are* the only qualified investigator in the room."

Brent wrinkled his nose. "If I had to guess, you're either trying to get your hands on half the fee, which I can tell you right now, isn't going to happen. Or, and admittedly this is an outside bet, you have some sort of weird alien crush on me, and you just had to come down and tell me to my face. Either way, you're fresh out of luck, so bon voyage, happy trails and all that, but basically, this is where we say our goodbyes and move on with our lives."

Rawlgeeb's smile vanished, but it was not replaced by the submissive grin that Brent had expected, nor did the Gloabon nod meekly and back away. Instead, Rawlgeeb pulled himself up to his full height, raising his arm to point an accusing finger at Brent's face. "Don't you dare talk to me like that. You *owe* me, Brent. Big time. And I'm the one who knows the mayor personally, remember?" Moving Breamell gently aside, Rawlgeeb advanced on Brent, his finger jabbing the air to punctuate his words. "How do you think Mayor Enderley will react when I tell him how *I* was the one who solved the case? What's he going to do when he finds out that *you* kept the money and made him look foolish for paying out? What will your life be worth then, Brent? How long do you think you'll last after I drop that little bombshell in the mayor's lap, huh?"

Brent pursed his lips, trying to drum up his usual air of obstinate defiance, but his poker face failed him, and he felt the blood drain from his cheeks. "I'm thinking that the mayor doesn't really need to know about this. Not ever. So maybe we can come to some sort of deal. What do you say, Rawlgeeb? We split the fee sixty-forty?"

Rawlgeeb shook his head, his flinty eyes locked on Brent. "I want more than that."

"All right, fifty-fifty." Brent hesitated. "Shit, it isn't the alien crush thing, is it? Only–"

"Stop talking," Rawlgeeb interrupted. "You just don't get it, do you, Brent? I came down here looking for a *job*. I figured I'd proved my worth, and strangely enough, I thought you might have the decency to take me on. After everything I've done, after all I've been through…" He dropped his arm. "I thought you were better than this, Brent. I looked up to you. And when you told me about the money, I thought it was ideal. That could've been my stake money, my buy-in. I wanted nothing more than to invest in our new partnership, to get this agency up on its feet, but *you*…you had to go and spoil everything. Well, here's what's going to happen–I'm going to leave, and as soon as I've got myself set up, I'll let you know where to send my money. *All* of it." He turned his back on Brent. "Come on, Breamell. We're leaving."

Vince and Maisie both began talking at once, both begging Rawlgeeb to stay, but he didn't seem to hear them. Breamell tugged at Rawlgeeb's coat, demanding answers to a series of increasingly shrill questions, but although Rawlgeeb raised his voice to reply, she didn't pause long enough to listen.

And into this hubbub, Doctor Cooper strolled with a large paper bag. "I have the doughnuts," he called out cheerily, then he did a double-take as if doubting whether he'd entered the right room.

"Enough!" Brent yelled, his voice loud enough to rattle

the window panes, and when the others fell silent, he stood, affecting a dignified pose. "Ladies, gentlemen, and Gloabons," he began. "I stand before you a changed man. Something very important has been said here today, and it has touched me deeply, though not, I hasten to add, inappropriately in any way. You see, I have a dream that we few, we happy few, will go forward this day, and for all the days that come after, and say that they may take our lands, but they will never take apart our band of brothers. For never, in the field of human cornflakes, has so much been owed by so many, despite the number of final demands that have been sent. And though we stand on the shoulders of giants, we are not afraid. For there is a tide in the affairs of men, and women, and Gloabons obviously, which will not be denied." He extended his arms wide with a flourish. "My fellow, er, beings, ask not, is this a Gloabon I see before me? Ask, what can I do to help him? Because we are all in the gutter, but some of us are looking for the stairs. So in that spirit of mutual support, let us focus on those important words that we heard in this room today. And those words, my friends, were these: I…have…the…doughnuts."

Brent bowed deeply then faced his audience, awaiting their applause, but when the others simply stared at him, stony-faced, he added, "That's all I got." He offered them an encouraging smile. "Listen, this is the part where you all cheer and everybody's happy. I mean, you did all hear the part where I said *doughnuts*, right?"

"We heard every word," Maisie said frostily. "We're just stunned by your utter pomposity."

"Thank you," Brent said, beaming. "It's a gift. I guess I'm just one of those people who have a way with the stringing together of words to make them sound real good."

Rawlgeeb stomped closer to Brent's desk, a low growl

escaping from between his clenched teeth. "It's *conflict*, Brent. Not *cornflakes*. *Human conflict*. C, O, N, F, L, I, C, T. *Conflict*."

"Jeez, I didn't know this was a spelling bee," Brent replied. "Still, I'm glad you picked up on my point. There's too much conflict in the room, and you know the real victim here? Those doughnuts. They're not getting any fresher, people, and unless I'm much mistaken, serving stale pastries is still a public health violation in this state."

"Oh, you're mistaken all right," Rawlgeeb said. "As usual."

Breamell stood beside Rawlgeeb on his right, Maisie on his left. All three faced Brent across his desk, their expressions bypassing stern completely and heading straight for outright condemnation.

"Tough crowd," Brent muttered.

"Believe it," Maisie replied. "You'd better apologize, Brent, and it had better make sense, or so help me, I might start using this." She scooped something up from Brent's desk, pointing it firmly at his chest.

Brent snorted. "Maisie, that's just a stapler. What are you going to do, clip my invoices to my final demands?"

"That's *not* a stapler," Breamell put in. "That happens to be a Kreitian Killzoid, the most powerful handgun in the galaxy."

Brent glared at Rawlgeeb. "Why, you deceitful little—"

"I told a white lie," Rawlgeeb interrupted. "So what? I'd do it again." He drew a steadying breath. "Listen, Brent, I'll give you one last chance. Play straight with me, or I might just show Maisie where the safety catch is on that thing."

"There's no need for all these threats," Brent said, sounding hurt. "I only mentioned the doughnuts because, and you're going to kick yourselves when you hear this, I was about to say that those little dollops of deep-fried carbohydrate are often highly important to an investigator, and you'll come to understand that, Rawlgeeb, when, with my help, you become a *fully qualified member of the Association of Galactic Investigators!*"

Rawlgeeb narrowed his eyes. "Are you serious? Because if this is more of your bullshit, I have to warn you that I'm fresh out of patience."

"I've never been more sure about anything in my life," Brent replied. "Apart from that system I had worked out for the lottery, but I was robbed by the corporate machine, man. They couldn't risk the truth leaking out, so they had to fix it."

"Brent!" Rawlgeeb warned.

Brent held up his hands. "All right. You got me. I was going to keep the mayor's money, okay? To be blunt, I needed the cash to keep this agency afloat, and I figured you'd be heading straight back to your swanky space station, Rawlgeeb. I honestly thought you'd never give this place a backward glance. And I figured, he doesn't want the money, so why shouldn't I use it to do some good? I was going to pay the rent on this joint and keep the lights on for a few months while I straightened the place out. And I'd have been able to finally give Vince all the back pay I owe him. Heck, I was even planning on getting Algernon the aquarium he so desperately needs. I mean, look at him, the poor little sucker. Look at that sad little face. He's all alone in the world. He really needs a break."

They all turned, looking from Algernon to Vince and back again.

Sensing their confusion, Brent added, "I meant *the fish*,

people, not Vince. Although, now that I think about it…"

"Hey!" Vince cried. "I've had enough of being talked to like some kind of idiot." He marched across the room to join Rawlgeeb. "Come on, let's go. We're wasting our time here." He threw a glare at Brent. "And don't worry, you don't even need to think about firing me. I quit!" He made a move toward the door, but Rawlgeeb grabbed hold of his arm, bringing him to a sudden halt.

"There's no need for you to leave, Vince," Rawlgeeb said. "You'll get your back pay, *and* you'll get a raise."

Vince looked as though he wanted to argue, but Rawlgeeb didn't give him the chance. "Things will be very different around here when I'm a partner in the business."

"Hold on, I didn't say anything about being partners," Brent put in. "I was thinking you'd be more of a freelance operative, know what I mean? No ties. In and out fast. Get the job done, then boom! You stride off into the night, walking down those mean streets alone, neither varnished nor afraid."

Rawlgeeb shook his head. "It's *tarnished*, T, A, R–"

Brent flapped his hands in the air. "Don't start that again. This is a detective agency, not an elementary school." He folded his arms. "All right. Let's talk turkey. If you really want to be a partner in this place, Rawlgeeb, we'll have to get a few things straight from the get-go."

Rawlgeeb nodded firmly. "I agree. We'll need to draw up a contract and go through the books, organize the budgets and set a few spending limits."

"Yeah, well, let's not go overboard," Brent said hurriedly. "One step at a time. You know Bolster's first law, right?"

"I think so, but go ahead," Rawlgeeb replied. "Surprise

me."

"It's simple enough–never make a deal on an empty stomach," Brent said. "You can get in a lot of trouble that way, as my former wife would testify. If you could find her."

"You were married?" Maisie asked.

Brent shrugged. "Only for as long as it took her to siphon off all my cash and destroy my sense of self-worth. Boy, that was a bad day." He shook his head to dispel the memory. "But let's not dwell on the past. I sense that this is a time for new beginnings. Vince, how about a little coffee to toast our new partnership? Wait, do we have decaf or something?"

"I doubt it," Vince replied. "Last time I looked there was nothing left but the Colombian Cardiac Resuscitation blend."

"Hell's teeth, don't give him that," Brent spluttered. "We don't need another interplanetary war on our hands–not yet anyway. Vince, could you be a sport and run down to the store and fetch something to drink for our Gloabon friends? Preferably something we can serve without needing riot gear afterward."

Vince didn't move. "Maybe. But listen, Brent, if I'm going to stay working here, I need some things to happen. I get that Rawlgeeb has a buy-in, and I'm totally cool with him jumping on the ladder to join the AGI, but I'm making that climb myself, remember? Seems like I've been sitting on the bottom rung for an awful long time, and that just isn't right."

Brent cast his eyes upward with a sigh, then he regarded Vince levelly, hoping to make him change his mind by the force of his stare alone. It didn't work.

"All right," Brent said, throwing his hands in the air. "I'll get your application started, er, I mean expedited. And we'll see what we can do to move it right along."

"I concur," Rawlgeeb chipped in. "And if all goes well, Vince, I don't see why you might not make partner yourself, in time."

Vince beamed. "Cool. Is there anything I can get you at the store, Mr. Rawlgeeb, sir? Would you like a soda or something?"

"No," Rawlgeeb replied with a grimace. "I can't tolerate those fizzy drinks."

"Is that another thing Gloabons can't digest?" Maisie asked.

Rawlgeeb shook his head. "No, but they make me belch, and you don't want to see a Gloabon do that. Trust me."

"All right, folks," Brent said, looking around the group. "We've got Vince and Rawlgeeb fixed up. Anybody else? Doc, are you about to express a sudden desire to throw your nine-to-five aside and embark on a thrilling new career as a private eye?"

"No!" Cooper blurted. "No, no, no. I've had more than enough of your particular brand of excitement." He shuddered. "I'll be heading back to work at the Institute, thank you very much."

"Your loss," Brent said. "Still, if we ever need a little scientific know-how, maybe we could call you up, huh? You know, for old times' sake."

"Or you could find someone else," Cooper offered. "In fact, yes, that would almost certainly be for the best. I think I'm having my contact number changed very soon, and we have tight security at GIT. Very tight. So it's probably safer if you stayed well away." He backed toward the door. "I must dash. I'll send someone around to fetch my gear. I have an urgent…thing to attend to. Goodbye. It's been…interesting."

"Won't you stay for coffee?" Maisie asked. "After all, you fetched the doughnuts."

Doctor Cooper paused in the doorway. "Enjoy them. My treat." He smiled at Maisie then disappeared into the hallway, and a second later, they heard his footsteps thumping down the stairs.

"Maisie, thanks for all your help," Brent said. "Being thrown in cells won't be the same without you, but I guess you'll be heading back to the UN." He shrugged. "I'm sure you won't want to hang around here."

"What makes you say that?" Maisie wiggled her eyebrows. "Maybe I want to be a private eye too."

Brent let out a dismissive snort. "No disrespect, Maisie, but you're just a wo–"

The weapon in Maisie's hand glowed bright, emitting a shrill whine, and an overpowering stench of scorched earth filled the room. Vince pointed dumbly at the wall, and when Brent looked over his shoulder, he spent a long second examining the circular hole that had been punched through the brickwork.

"Oops! I'm such a woolly-headed girl," Maisie said. "But I guess I figured out this advanced piece of alien hardware all by my silly old self."

"Fair point," Brent admitted, looking Maisie in the eye. "But while the new hole lets in some much-needed light, the Feng Shui in this room is all shot to hell. Quite literally."

"You had it coming." Maisie lowered her aim. "So what was it you were saying?"

"Only that you're just a *wonderful* asset to the community with your incredibly valuable job at the UN," Brent replied.

"And naturally, I assumed you'd be heading back to your fancy office and your high-powered buddies at the first opportunity." He gestured to the wall. "Still, I'll always have something to remember you by."

Maisie narrowed her eyes. "I don't believe that's what you were really going to say—not for one second—but you're right about one thing. I *am* going back to my job, so I guess I won't be needing this." She laid the weapon down on Brent's desk, and when it let out a buzz, everyone flinched.

"Don't worry," Breamell put in. "It just needs recharging." She let out a long breath, puffing out her cheeks. "You know, I'm trying hard to play catch-up here, but I can't see where *I* fit in." She looked sadly at Rawlgeeb. "I thought you were going places in the administration, Rawlgeeb, but now it looks like you're not the Gloabon I thought you were. And it seems that you're prepared to throw all your hard work away and abandon your old life. Is that true? Are you really leaving *The Gamulon* for good?"

Rawlgeeb stiffened his spine. "I don't see that I have much choice, Breamell, but, you know, sometimes, the problems of two Gloabons don't amount to a hill of beans, and you have your work. It's important work. The administration will need you to help sort this mess out. The paperwork alone…" He ran his hand over his smooth scalp. "The truth is, I don't think I can ask you stay here with me–it would be asking you to leave too much behind. And I can't do that, Breamell. I…I think too highly of you." He hesitated. "But, remember, Breamell, we'll always have the space dock. We'll always have pier twelve."

Breamell nodded sadly. "I think I'd better be going. Maisie, perhaps we could head out together."

"Of course." Maisie cast an appraising glance at

Rawlgeeb then wrapped her arm around Breamell's shoulder and guided her toward the door. "Goodbye, Vince, Brent," she said. "Good luck, Rawlgeeb. I hope it all works out."

Rawlgeeb gave Breamell a tiny wave, but as she left the room with Maisie, Rawlgeeb looked down at the floor as if lost in thought.

"That leaves just the three of us," Brent said brightly. "More doughnuts to go around. Rawlgeeb, grab a seat. Vince, if you could be quick with fetching that decaf, that would be great."

Doctor Cooper had set the bag of doughnuts down on the corner of Vince's desk, and Brent hurried over to retrieve them. He peered inside before offering the bag to Rawlgeeb. "You'd better have the first choice. You look like you need it."

Rawlgeeb nodded sadly and sat down carefully on the visitors' chair, taking a doughnut from the bag without looking inside. "Thank you," he murmured, and when he bit into the sugar-coated snack, he smiled bravely. "This is very…soft. No scales."

Brent patted him on the shoulder. "Attaboy. A couple of those and you'll feel better. Bloated, but better."

Vince made to leave, but he paused before reaching the door and looked around the office as if seeing it for the first time. Only one occupant of the room made eye contact, and Vince returned the impassive stare. "Well, Algernon," Vince said, glancing at Brent and Rawlgeeb, "this looks like being the start of a weird friendship. A very weird friendship indeed."

EPILOGUE

Aboard *The Kreltonian Skull* - Andromeda Class Battle Cruiser

Official Status: Returned to the Andel-Kreit fleet-awaiting deployment orders.

Ship's Log: Earth Orbit.

The woman gasped as she opened her eyes. The room was dimly lit with a gentle, pink glow, but although the bed she found herself on was soft and warm, a memory of the cold and dark still clung to her consciousness, and she shivered. Her hands flew to her face, and she whispered, "Oh my God! Oh my God!"

"It's all right," a velvety voice murmured, and the woman sat up, hugging her knees to her chest, her fingers curled into fists.

"Who are you?" she demanded. "Where the hell am I?"

From the shadows in the corner of the room, a tall figure emerged, its posture upright. It stopped a few feet from her bed and held up a hand in greeting. "My name is Zeb, and I shall be your relocation officer today. You have been in a deep sleep inside a vessel of the Andel-Kreit coalition fleet, however, it is my job to prepare you for the return journey to your home on Earth. Do you understand?"

The woman shook her head. "No! No, I don't. What happened?"

"Allow me to explain." The strange figure came closer, and she saw that Zeb was some sort of cyborg, but although the sight shook her, there was something in cyborg's manner that quietened her fears. "You were taken by the Globons," Zeb went on. "Unfortunately, a rogue Andelian admiral diverted you to his ship for reasons that we won't go into right now because, frankly, they would scare the hell out of you. However, to cut a long story short, you've been rescued, and now it's time for you to go home." Zeb held out his hands as though further explanation was unnecessary. "The Commander in Chief of the Andel-Kreit Fleet has authorized me to issue a full apology, and of course, you will be fully reimbursed for any loss of earnings you have incurred. Regrettably, the time you've spent asleep aboard our vessel cannot be returned to you, but don't worry, you will not be charged for storage or life support, and your journey home will be paid for by the Gloabon Government." Zeb lowered his voice. "You'll need to fill in a form about that later I'm afraid, but that's the Gloabons for you."

"I just…want to go home," the woman murmured.

"Of course you do," Zeb said cheerfully. "In fact, if you could just lie down and shut your eyes for a second, we'll be able to send you on your way, all right?" He nodded encouragingly. "Sorry for the rush, madam, but quite honestly, I have a hell of a lot more humans to get through before I finish my shift, so if you wouldn't mind…" He made a downward gesture. "Lie down, please. It's almost time and we're on a strict schedule."

"Why do I have to lie down?" the woman demanded. "Hey! What's ha–"

The woman vanished and Zeb took a few steps back and pressed a button on the wall. With a soft hiss, the empty bed retracted and slid back out again a moment later, this time with a man on the mattress. "Next!" Zeb called out, stepping back into the shadows.

The man opened his eyes, and with a gasp, he took a deep breath.

Thank You for reading Dial G for Gravity

I hope that you enjoyed it.

Want more like this? Please consider leaving a review.

Reviews are a great way of encouraging authors to write more in a series or a genre, so if you'd like more books like this, your review will support the development of new books. Even a short review will help.

Thank you.

Special thanks go to Netty and Saundra who were very kind in checking for typos and found the ones that no one else could spot. Thank you.

The Awkward Squad

The Home of Picky Readers

All members receive a newsletter worth reading plus Compendium, a starter collection of exclusive previews. You'll also receive bonus content and advance notice of regular discounts and free books

Join at:

mikeycampling.com/freebooks

Coming Soon

Brent Bolster in

Dead Men Don't Disco

New books are coming out all the time.

Don't Miss Out

The best way to keep up to date with Michael's new releases is to sign up for his newsletter at:

mikeycampling.com/freebooks

Also by Michael Campling

One url to Rule Them All: michaelcampling.com

Brent Bolster Space Detective

Dial G for Gravity

Dead Men Don't Disco

The Surrana Identity

Double Infinity

The Downlode Trust Series:

C0NTINUE? - A Downlode Trust Prequel

CHEATC0DE - The Downlode Trust Book I

The Trust - The Downlode Trust Book II

Colony B Series:

Skeleton Crew - A Colony B Prequel

Wall - Colony B Book I

Trail - Colony B Book II

Control - Colony B Book III

Rift - Colony B Book IV

The Darkeningstone Series:

Breaking Ground - A Darkeningstone Prequel

Trespass: The Darkeningstone Book I

Outcast—The Darkeningstone Book II

Scaderstone—The Darkeningstone Book III

The Short Horror Collection

After Dark - Thoughtful Horror Book I

Once in a Blood Moon - Thoughtful Horror Book II

A Dark Assortment - Thoughtful Horror Book III

Other Fiction

The God Machine

Changes

Destinly's Hand

Prison Quest

Anthologies

Uprising: 12 Dystopian Futures

The Expanding Universe 3

The Expanding Universe 4

About the Author

Michael (Mikey to friends) is a full-time writer living and working in a tiny village on the edge of Dartmoor in Devon. He writes stories with characters you can believe in and plots you can sink your teeth into.

Michael's work spans several genres, and you can get a flavor of the range with Compendium, a starter collection you'll receive when you join Michael's readers' group, The Awkward Squad. You'll get a newsletter that's actually worth reading, and you'll receive advance notice of regular discounts and free books.

Learn more and start reading today via Mikey's blog, because everyone ought to be awkward once in a while: mikeycampling.com/freebooks

Copyright

Printed in Poland
by Amazon Fulfillment
Poland Sp. z o.o., Wrocław

50127374R00141